ENGRAVE DANGER

A CHARM ISLAND MYSTERY
BOOK 1

CASEY GRIFFIN

CHARMING FROG
PUBLISHING

For all the folks I met on Haida Gwaii

CHAPTER ONE

As I waited at the ferry terminal, where my ride to Charm Island lurked in the Pacific waters, I hugged myself, and it wasn't because of the crisp morning air but from nerves. My return would make several laps around the gossip circuit by suppertime, and I hoped to make it home without running into someone I knew from my past life. Or, more importantly, the afterlife.

It was the first departure of the day, and dawn was dragging its feet. The heavy cloud cover didn't help either. At least the gloom concealed me from the familiar faces already boarding. I stood back and waited until the deckhands scrambled and the ship looked ready to cast off.

Struggling into the straps of my enormous backpack, I marched across the passenger walkway. A man in a captain's hat stood ramrod straight by the entrance. He greeted me with a nod and held out his hand for my ticket.

I hesitated. But what choice did I have? I was there to help Dad recover from his accident. Nothing was more important. Not my past, my shame, or my fear of what waited for me at the end of the ferry ride. He'd get better eventually, then I'd return to Europe. Or maybe I'd explore South America. Any place that wasn't Charm Island, because it was better off without me.

"Last call for passengers!" The wiry deckhand threw me an impatient look from behind his shaggy hair. "Coming aboard? Or are you planning to swim?"

The captain's weathered skin wrinkled with a smile as he gestured for my ticket again. He was probably used to the deckhand's snarky attitude.

I pulled out my phone and brought up the one-way ticket for the old captain to scan. Head tilted, he stared at the screen with a hole punch in his hand. A few awkward seconds passed before I took in the mutton chops blending with his handlebar mustache and realized my mistake: he'd died long before electronic tickets were a thing. Or cell phones, for that matter. Like a reluctant retiree, he'd not been ready to leave his post, even as a ghost.

I berated myself for not noticing before. In the five years since my curse had begun, I'd become pretty good at identifying lingering spirits and subsequently avoiding them. However, dim light always made it trickier.

The deckhand cleared his throat and jiggled the handheld scanner. "You need to hold it out for me to actually scan it."

I rubbed the back of my neck. "Sorry. I was just taking a video."

Cheeks burning, I pretended to record the scenic car ramp and rusty ship hull before letting him scan my phone. Ignoring his probing look, I boarded the ferry.

Only two vehicles were parked on board. One of them was a pearl-colored luxury SUV. Nice ride for something that would be lucky to rack up a thousand miles a year on Charm Island. Most people didn't even own a car, since everything in town was within walking distance. A vehicle like that was more of an expensive lawn ornament to announce your status than a mode of transport.

I'd barely stowed my backpack on the luggage rack before

a horn blast reverberated through the air. The metal deck juddered beneath me as the engine rumbled to life. Chest tightening, I turned back to the land slowly slipping away and resisted the urge to jump overboard.

As the vessel departed without its old captain, he shouted and appeared tempted to swim after us. Considering the gestures he was making, I was glad I couldn't hear spirits. He didn't dive in, of course. Ghosts hated water. Since they couldn't affect their surroundings, I assumed that applied to the doggy paddle, so maybe they'd sink right to the bottom and remain stuck there like a rock.

I shuddered at the idea, yet I was grateful for this quirk. Their fear of water was the reason I'd been able to leave my past behind five years ago.

After turning my back on the man doomed to forevermore miss the boat, literally and metaphorically, I climbed the stairs to the second deck. The clouds sagging with moisture finally sprang a leak, and the wind hurled a light drizzle against my cheeks like tiny daggers.

I slipped on my jacket hood and thought about waiting it out to avoid going inside. As the saying went, if you don't like the weather along the Lunar Coast, wait five minutes. But it didn't look as though it would let up anytime soon, and I'd be soaked by the end of the trip. Sighing, I opened the metal door to the covered area and snuck inside.

A handful of passengers occupied the rows of colorful plastic chairs. Once the weather warmed and the tourists took over the island, the space would be standing room only. For now, it was quiet enough that I might make the journey unnoticed. That's when a red peacoat over zebra-print leggings caught my eye, and I recognized the outfit's owner as Lucy Litton, the town busybody-turned-reporter.

The blond bombshell sat in the corner, angled to keep one eye on the goings-on around her and the other on a fashion magazine. Her sense of style still matched her larger-than-life personality—or maybe it was just larger than what our sleepy town was used to. In high school, we'd all thought she'd end up in Hollywood, hosting one of those celebrity-gossip TV shows, but she'd stuck around the island to work at the local newspaper, *The Siren*.

Before she noticed me, I adjusted my hood to cover my telltale red hair and took a seat at the back. I'd barely settled in when the door to the outer deck opened, and a gust of cold air rushed over me. Shivering, I automatically glanced up and wished I hadn't.

My would-have-been father-in-law swept a calculating gaze over the deck's occupants until it landed on me. His presence likely explained the overpriced SUV on the lower deck. I regretted not jumping overboard when I'd had the chance. However, after Quinton Abernathy did a double take my way, his expression twisted into one that said he'd happily rectify that for me.

He ran a hand over his rain-dampened hair and strode my way. "Violet, you're back."

I wasn't sure what I'd been expecting. A "nice to see you." A "how have you been?" At least his response was a step up from "I wish *you* would have died in the accident," which was the last thing he'd said to me before I'd left. So this was progress.

I stood so he couldn't look down his long, straight nose at me. "Hello, Mr. Abernathy. It's been a long time."

"That's *Mayor* Abernathy, if you don't mind. We didn't think you were going to return." His tone made it sound like they'd hoped I wouldn't.

Digging my nails into my palms, I smiled. "The island is still my home. I'm back because my father broke his arm a few days ago, and he needs help running the family business."

He smirked. "How is his little bauble shop?"

My smile faltered at the obvious slight. He knew perfectly well that we sold high-end jewelry. "Good, actually. We've recently started selling pieces I've secured from throughout Europe." I tried to make it sound highly exclusive.

Abernathy's lip curled. "As they say, one man's trash is another man's treasure." He gave me the once-over.

Yeah, I got it. I was the trash.

"Well, I hope your business won't keep you in town for long. I wish your father a speedy recovery."

No doubt his concern was less about Dad and more about when I'd be on my way. Finished with the pleasantries, he brushed past me.

Part of me wanted to live the rest of my days in Hope City just to spite him and his wife. But our meeting probably wasn't a nostalgic experience for him either. After all, if it hadn't been for me, his son Nolan would still be alive. Sure, I hadn't been the one to tamper with his car before our accident—not that anybody believed my recounting of how it had lost control. Whoever had done that was still running around, a free person. However, it was because of me that we were even on the road that night, rounding a treacherous corner.

I was about to drop back into my seat when I caught Lucy's laser focus on me, drawn by the whiff of drama in the air. Before she could pounce, I made a break for the exit.

The second I shoved open the metal door, cool droplets pelted my skin. The weather hadn't improved. Sheets of rain rippled in the wind gusts, while the muted light and fog blended the dreary sky and dark waters into one. And yet I was determined to suffer through the rest of the journey outside.

Following the walkway around, I searched for a covering or alcove. I would have even settled for a restroom. When I drew closer to the ship's bow, I found a nook beneath a set of stairs and took cover there. Pulling my jacket tighter around me, I leaned back against the wall.

My eyelids drooped. I'd left Italy the morning before—or would it be the night before?—and I was going on thirty-six hours of travel. All I wanted to do was get home, hug my dad, and crash.

Just as I dozed off, I heard yelling on the deck above me.

"We're not done talking!"

The male voice growled with anger, but I recognized it like I'd recognize my own. It had spoken a million words to me in friendship and comfort, whispered countless secrets and inside jokes. The last time I'd heard it, though, the night before I was to wed his best friend, it had spoken of love. For me.

The voice belonged to Max Nicolas.

CHAPTER TWO

Two pairs of footsteps thudded down the stairs above my hiding spot until my old friend Max and the deckhand with the floppy hair came into view. Curious, I peered between a gap in the metal steps.

The deckhand sneered. "You can't come here and harass me while I'm at work. We'll talk about this tonight."

Max shoved him against the wall. "You've been avoiding me, so we'll talk about this now."

"Okay, okay." The deckhand shrank as though he wished the wall would open up and swallow him. "I guess I can spare a minute."

Max's aggression surprised me, making me even more nervous about seeing him again. I stayed put, hoping the men were just passing by. Wide-eyed, I drank in the lines of my old friend's vexed profile, with his square jaw and long, would-be straight nose that had healed a bit crooked after a fight in our senior year.

Because of his size, other guys had always picked fights with him to prove how tough they were. Spoiler alert: they weren't. However, while Max was as fierce as a bear when he needed to be, he reminded me of the cuddly, stuffed kind deep down. Watching him now, though, it seemed the years had replaced some of that stuffing with grit.

Max crossed his arms. "We had a deal, Christian. What happened?"

The wiry man tried to stand tall even while cowering. "What do you mean? I still have two weeks to pay you."

"That was before you decided to leave the island." Max spoke calmly, but it was almost more intimidating that way. "Don't bother denying it. It's a small town, and I've seen the ads for your furniture posted around the promenade. You're going to pay me before you leave, or I will hunt you down."

Christian's Adam's apple bobbed. "You'll get your money in five days."

"Three."

"All right. Three." He straightened his collar. "Now, let me get back to work. If you get me fired, you won't see any money."

"We'll hammer out the details tonight." Max pointed a warning finger at him before sauntering away.

Christian raked his fingers through his hair, only for it to flop back in front of his eyes. After a scan for witnesses, he stalked down the walkway with a measured pace that ensured he wouldn't catch up to Max.

Feeling like a sitting duck, I moved to leave my hiding spot then caught zebra print out of the corner of my eye and froze. Lucy slunk by and peeked around the corner where the shake-down had occurred. Finding the coast clear, she snuck after the two men.

Had she been searching for me when she'd stumbled onto that scene? Hopefully, the scent of fresh blood in the air would throw her off my track. In the meantime, I needed to find a quieter place to hide.

I slipped out of my nook and tiptoed up the staircase the men had descended. It led to an open deck, but at least the rain had stopped. From this height, I had a three-sixty view of the ferry and the dark waters of Prosper Strait. I watched the undulating waves as I considered what I'd just witnessed.

The tough-guy persona wasn't a new thing for Max, but I understood him enough to tell he'd been serious. What had happened to my teddy bear?

I gripped the metal railing. Maybe I looked like I was about to crawl over and go for a swim, because a man nearby interrupted my racing thoughts.

"You all right?"

Startled, I spun toward him. Who was it now?

A middle-aged man in a navy rain jacket leaned against the opposite railing. He wore a captain's hat, and I assumed he was the current one this time. I looked past the three-day scruff on his jaw. Thankfully, I didn't recognize him.

"I'm fine," I lied. For the first time, I noticed the enclosed cabin with tinted windows. It must have been the captain's bridge. "Is it okay that I'm up here?"

"Usually, it's just me and the helmsman allowed. Why? Want a better seat to watch the show from?" His mouth twisted with a wry smirk.

I blinked. He meant the fight. "I didn't mean to eavesdrop. I was looking for some peace and quiet."

His chuckle was a rich rumble, not unlike the hum of the engine. "I don't blame you. I'm sick and tired of those two bickering on my ship as if it's poker night."

"Does it happen often?" I asked, wondering more about Max than Christian.

"More often than I'd like. I run a tight ship, so nothing happens without me knowing."

Apparently, that applied to spotting eavesdroppers too.

He took off his hat and scratched his head with the brim before replacing it. "That deckhand causes more trouble than he's worth sometimes. But it's hard to find good workers."

Ahead of us, a land mass blanketed in old-growth forest emerged from the water like a raw emerald. Charm Island.

The mountain range at its center dipped and swelled, emulating the voluptuous contours of a woman lying on her side. While it probably had an official name, everyone called her Sleeping Beauty.

Home sweet home.

I thrust my chin at our destination. "Speaking of working, shouldn't you be steering the boat?"

"I have a helmsman for that. But we'll be arriving soon, so I'll leave you to your peace and quiet. Enjoy your time on the island." On his way inside the bridge, he gestured toward the front of the deck. "The view is better from over there."

"Thanks."

He disappeared inside, and I followed his suggestion. He'd been right about the view. It was the best seat in the house to survey the colorfully painted shops and restaurants clinging to the cliffs. The red-and-white lighthouse perched on the rocks still reminded me of a stick of candy.

Two great headlands jutted out into the sea, protective arms creating a natural harbor on either side of Hope City. Well, "city" was a stretch. It was technically a village. Back when it was first established, it had been called a city to trick people into moving there. It didn't work, but the name stuck.

A mysterious air hung about the place, one I'd never noticed during all my years growing up there. Seeing it now, with fresh eyes, conjured questions I'd been suppressing for some time. Questions about the existence of magic and the beings who might wield it. If such things were real, I supposed they would be hidden in a place like Charm Island. But that was a big "if," because I didn't want to believe it. Ghosts were enough for me, thanks.

The captain—or the helmsman—pulled into the ferry slip, and I eyed the pier running next to it, where two men waited for the ship's arrival. Despite the distance, there was no mistaking the man in the three-piece suit with perfectly styled honey-colored hair. My fiancé.

As though Nolan sensed me, his gaze locked on mine. I was slapped by a sense of déjà vu. He stood in the exact spot I'd left him, like he hadn't moved since the day I'd run away five years ago. Thanks to the cloud cover, he looked as alive and handsome as he had the night of our rehearsal dinner. The night he'd died.

While enough time had gone by that I didn't burst into tears at the sight of him, I felt the past settle heavily onto my shoulders. I tore my focus away from him, more eager than ever to get home. After racing down to the lower deck, I grabbed my backpack and beelined it for the passenger gate, only to find it still locked, the ship not fully secured yet.

Footsteps clanged on the metal stairs from the enclosed deck, and passengers lined up behind me. I kept my eyes trained forward, hoping no one would recognize me. But it wasn't long before my name rose above the chatter.

And so the gossip begins.

What had I been thinking? I should have held back until everyone else had disembarked. Shifting from foot to foot, I waited for the deckhands to let us off.

Unable to resist, I checked the pier again. Nolan was watching me. Surely, he didn't expect me to stop and greet him. Facing my dead fiancé on my first day back wasn't on my itinerary. While it felt cruel to ignore him, I couldn't hear ghosts anyway, and I wasn't even sure they understood me. Besides, talking to thin air in front of people would only kick up a torrent of rumors.

Not far from Nolan, another man waited to meet someone. Or else he was just early for the next departure. Gloved hands shoved into the pockets of his mustard-yellow work jacket, he scowled at the water below.

I followed his gaze to where bits of garbage littered the water's surface: plastic bottles, a potato chip bag, beer cans, and something else… fabric.

My name pierced the air again, louder this time. "Violet?" It was Max.

I pretended not to hear over the water lapping and engine idling. Partly because I wasn't ready to face him yet. I needed time, rest, and a toothbrush. But more importantly, I was fixated on the fabric in the water.

A shirt? No. A jacket, like the one the grumpy man on the pier wore. As I continued to stare, I spotted two gloves floating on either side of it. A pair of boots bobbed in the water, completing the morbid outfit.

Fingers snapped in front of my face, dragging my attention back. Christian glared at me like I was simple. "You can go now."

People jostled impatiently behind me, but I remained rooted to the spot. With a shaking finger, I pointed at the water.

"Is that…?"

Before I could finish the sentence, my mind filled in the rest of the image. A pair of jeans nearly blended into the water, and tendrils of dark hair fanned out over the jacket's collar.

A woman behind me gasped. "Someone's in the water. Call an ambulance!"

But I already knew it was too late to save him, because the grumpy man on the pier wasn't there to meet the ferry. He was the ghost of the man floating in the water, waiting to meet his maker.

CHAPTER THREE

Above the ferry terminal, birds chirped while floating on the briny sea breeze, indifferent to the tarp at the bottom of the ramp hiding the poor soul. Well, it was hiding his body. The actual soul was still watching events unfold from the pier, as sulky as ever. Not that I blamed him.

Since everything in Hope was only a five-minute drive away, the ambulance had arrived quickly. However, once it had pulled up, the EMTs didn't spend long with the victim before their attention shifted to the captain, the brave hero who'd jumped in and swum the body to shore. Now, he sat in the back of the ambulance, wrapped in blankets, while the sheriff spoke with him.

Waiting for my turn to be questioned, I stood near the edge of the platform, away from the other commuters huddled beneath the sloped roof. I was overly aware of the ghost stomping back and forth along the pier. His mouth moved silently as he yelled and gestured wildly, perhaps angry no one was attempting to revive him. I didn't want to dwell on what made the EMTs decide there was no use trying.

Being a new ghost must have been bewildering. Nolan seemed to have a handle on it, though. Unlike the last time I'd seen him, he wasn't lurking in dark corners, screaming silently in my face when I was in public, or trying to kiss me. Cool as a sea cucumber, he leaned against one of the pier's tall pillars, hands in his pockets, as though he sensed this wasn't the best time for a reunion.

While I eyed my fiancé, a small black cat emerged from the shadows to slink in a circle around him. No. Not a circle. It was coiling around his legs—or at least trying to.

But that couldn't be right. Did animals have a sixth sense for spirits? Although I'd never seen anything like it before, it wasn't as if I'd taken the time to study ghosts. In fact, I did everything I could to avoid them. They were just another reminder of the accident and those awful days following it when Nolan had haunted me. Most of the time, I pretended spirits were a figment of my imagination. Hey, no one ever said denial was healthy, but it was the only reason I'd survived the last five years.

As I watched, the feline reminded me of Nolan's old cat, Zelda. She'd been an odd animal, walking him to school like a faithful dog and meeting him afterward as though she could tell time. But while the resemblance between the two cats was uncanny, they couldn't possibly be the same one. Zelda had been alive when I started dating Nolan in junior year, and this one seemed too young and frisky to be her. Then again, I'd faced stranger things than an immortal pet, like ghosts or when Nolan had claimed to be a warlock, yet another memory I'd worked hard to suppress.

The black cat padded over to me. After a wary sniff of my backpack resting beside me on the wooden planks, she sneezed.

I rolled my eyes. "Yeah, I know. I have some laundry to do. Don't judge me." When Dad had called with the news of his tumble down the stairs, I'd thrown everything into my bag and grabbed the next available flight home from Italy.

The feline sat directly in front of me and meowed loudly

until I picked her up. Scratching her head, I checked for a collar then her ear for a tattoo. Nothing.

"Where did you come from, little one?"

I ran a hand over her silky flank. She was well fed. In any other place, I would have worried, but in Hope, pets didn't get lost. They went on outings. Vehicles were a rarity, making traffic a nonissue, and an abundance of deer in the mountains kept predators busy.

"Yoo-hoo! Violet!" sang a nasally voice. Lucy Litton.

"Save me," I pleaded with my new friend.

The cat purred and settled against me. It looked like I was on my own.

Mustering a smile, I faced the gossip queen headed toward me. "Lucy. It's been a minute."

"It has, hasn't it?" She wrinkled her nose at the animal in my arms. "Is that your cat?"

"No." I didn't bother to explain.

"You always were a strange one, Woods." She stood next to me, her bright red coat too cheerful for the solemn occasion.

Not in the mood to navigate a conversational minefield, I checked the time on my phone. Nine a.m. Dad would be wondering where I was. However, I must have been standing in one of the many roving dead spots on the island because I had no service. It was a running joke between locals, who would invent increasingly ridiculous excuses: the low-hanging clouds, the gentle breeze, the upcoming full moon, and the list went on.

Holding my phone in the air, I turned it this way and that to search for a signal. The bars didn't so much as flicker. I hoped the sheriff would hurry and question me next so I could leave, but he was still talking to the captain.

Lucy clicked her tongue. "What a sad situation." But the twinkle in her green eyes said this was the hottest scoop since… well, since the accident that had changed my life and taken Nolan's. "I was in the little girls' room and missed everything.

Quite the coincidence how trouble turns up the moment you do. Maybe you were a black cat in a past life."

My feline friend meowed, taking offense.

Lucy was one to talk. She'd been sneaking around, spying on Max and Christian. So what if I stumbled upon drama? She hunted for it.

"You're right," I said. "It is a coincidence, considering I was probably somewhere over the Atlantic Ocean when the man died. I only came back to help my dad after his accident."

Lucy tilted her head, a crease forming between her perfectly sculpted eyebrows. "Accident?" Before she could say anything else, something over my shoulder caught her eye. "Oh, don't look now. Here comes Jason Swan. Ever since he became deputy, he struts around like he's the town hero or something."

Ignoring her suggestion, I looked. While I didn't see the awkward young man I remembered anywhere, I did notice the romance-book-cover version of a deputy strolling our way. Jason's complexion had cleared up, and his hunched lumber of a shy and too-tall boy had relaxed into a confident stride.

He flicked up the brim of his hat so the light caught the smooth planes of his angular face—"chiseled" was the word that popped into my head, like the rest of him. Jason Swan might have been a late bloomer, but he was all grown now.

Lucy snorted, clearly not as impressed as I was. "Remember that huge crush he had on you in high school?"

Heat prickled my cool cheeks. "I wouldn't say crush, exactly."

As Jason approached, his walk shifted into an easy swagger. "Violet Woods." He said my name like he was savoring it. "You're under arrest."

"W-What?" So much for that crush.

Even the cat jerked awake. She raised her head to level him with a cool look, not that cats had many other looks. Though she was likely just concerned about losing her warm nap spot in my arms.

He grinned, and a hint of his silly younger self peeked through. "I've always wanted to say that. I got assigned to the deputy position a few years back and haven't seen anything more exciting than a DUI. And since this is Charm Island, it wasn't even a car. It was a bicycle." He seemed way too pumped until he eyed the tarp. "But this wasn't what I had in mind for excitement on the job, you know?"

"So, I'm not arrested?"

"Not unless you killed the guy," he joked then stiffened. "Did you? Kill him, I mean?"

"N-No."

His shoulders deflated. "I guess it can't be that easy."

"Sorry to disappoint you." I didn't know the correct response to not having killed someone.

Lucy clapped him on the back. "Keep up the good work, Sherlock. I feel so much safer knowing you're on the case."

He swung around to face her. "Wait a minute. Lucy, what are you still doing here? I've already interviewed you."

"I'm here in my official capacity now." Producing a lanyard from her purse, she flashed her press credentials like a police badge.

Jason crossed his arms. "You can't just stroll around here. This is an active crime scene."

I gaped at him. "Crime scene? So the murder thing wasn't a joke? You really think someone killed him?"

Tensing, he glanced in the sheriff's direction. "I probably shouldn't have said that. Do me a favor and keep that to yourself, would you? I don't want to be back on desk duty." He pointed at Lucy. "And that goes double for you. It's off the record."

She smiled coyly, not making any promises. "This looks more like our annual garden tour than a crime scene. Security is pretty relaxed. Where's the caution tape?"

His brows knit together. "I haven't had a chance to put it up."

"Come to think of it," I said, "we were told to stick around. If a crime has been committed, why are people leaving before you've questioned them?"

"No police tape, I suspect," Lucy stage whispered.

Jason flung his arms up in exasperation. "For crying out loud. Who left?"

I scanned the passengers scattered around the terminal but didn't need to. I'd known the moment Max made himself scarce, because a wave of relief had washed over me.

Petting the cat in my arms, I avoided Jason's gaze. "A few people."

"Figures. No respect." He scrubbed a hand over his face.

Lucy held her phone up in front of him, recording a video. "Why do you suspect it was a murder and not an accidental drowning?"

He gave her a flat "no comment" look.

She rolled her eyes and put away her phone. "Right. Look who I'm talking to. You're just the deputy. If I want to know anything important, I should ask the sheriff."

It was obvious she was egging him on. Yet his pinched expression said it worked.

Raising his chin, he rocked back on his heels. "If it was an accident, there wouldn't be rope marks around his neck, now would there? It's a pretty dead giveaway."

I winced at his choice of words. "You mean someone strangled him? That's so awful."

He let out a frustrated groan and squeezed his eyes shut. "Don't tell anyone I said that either." He glared at Lucy. "I mean it. Not a word. Now, it's time you left or, so help me, I will arrest you."

She heaved a dramatic sigh. "Fine. I imagine you want to catch up on old times with this one, anyway." With a suggestive wink at me, she twirled around and sashayed away from the terminal.

Shaking his head, Jason turned back to me. "How are you doing? It must have been a shock to find the body." His shoulders shifted uncomfortably, like he was suppressing a shiver.

"It was." I noticed his continued discomfort. "Are you okay?"

"It's just a lot. I've never seen anyone… you know."

For all his lightheartedness earlier, now that we were alone, his bravado slipped away. He'd always been a jokester, especially during tough times. It must have been stressful to face his first death. If only it had been mine.

"Did you know him?" I asked.

"I'm not sure. The body hasn't been identified yet." He lowered his voice even though we were alone. "In all honesty, I'm afraid to look under the tarp."

I shuddered and held my furry friend closer to my chest. "I don't blame you. It wasn't a pretty sight, even from a distance."

Jason pointed to the feline, who was listening to our conversation with mild interest. "Is that your cat?"

"No." I figured wanting to snuggle with a cat, even an unfamiliar one, needed no explanation.

He regained some brownie points with me when he didn't ask for one. "I'm sorry you had such a terrible welcome home. What are the chances? Nothing like this has happened since…" His brow furrowed, and his focus dropped to his boots. "I'm sorry about what happened to Nolan. I wanted to come by after the accident and see how you were doing, but you left the island pretty quickly."

As though my eyes had a mind of their own, they found Nolan's ghost again. "Thanks. I guess I just needed a change of scenery."

Jason kicked a stray pebble. "Nolan was the reason I joined law enforcement. The strange circumstances around his death and the investigation… There was just something off about it, you know? It haunted me."

He was haunted? "Am I going to be questioned soon? I have to leave."

"Oh, right. That part." He pulled out his notepad and pen.

I blinked. "You're interviewing me? Not the sheriff?"

"I'm perfectly capable of asking questions." His face crumpled. "I'm an officer of the law, too, you know."

Lucy must have pushed one too many buttons. Or maybe it was more than just her. Jason's young-adult years had been rocky. I imagined after he'd grown up making every mistake in the book, stepping up as deputy had to be a tough transition in the locals' eyes. While I liked Jason, even I struggled to take him seriously.

Laying a hand on his arm, I squeezed reassuringly. "I didn't mean it like that. I'm relieved it's you. The sheriff and I aren't exactly BFFs."

Cheeks turning rosy, he dove into his questions. He didn't have many, since I'd only arrived in town that morning. When he asked if I'd witnessed anything strange on board the ferry, Max's fight with the deckhand came to mind. However, they'd been arguing about money, not a dead man.

In the end, I didn't mention it. Perhaps it was because of the ingrained loyalty I felt, but this was Max we were talking about. It wasn't like he'd killed the guy. Besides, he'd been returning from the mainland, so he wouldn't have been around at the time of death. Right?

I peeked at Jason's notes, half expecting to see a doodle. "Are we almost done?"

"Almost." He angled his notebook away, but not before I glimpsed a stick figure. "What brings you back here?"

"My dad."

Cringing, he clicked his pen closed. "That's right. How is he doing? The sheriff said he was in rough shape when he took his statement."

"Statement?" I gave a weak laugh. "What is the sheriff going to do? Arrest the broken stair he tripped on?"

He cocked his head and assessed me, not unlike Lucy had before we'd been interrupted. "Is that what he told you happened? Vi, your dad didn't fall. He had the tar beat out of him."

The platform beneath me seemed to tilt, and I staggered to one side. With a snarled meow, the cat leaped out of my arms, clearly not trusting my balance. Not trusting it either, I gripped Jason's shoulder.

"What?" I breathed. "By who?"

"A man named Wyatt Thorn." His eyes widened. "Oops. I'm not sure I was supposed to tell you that, either. Please don't let on to the sheriff that I told you."

I gave him a shake. "What happened?"

"Wyatt robbed Charming Treasures. Your dad was working late and caught him in the act. It was a wrong place, wrong time situation. Don't worry, we'll catch the guy."

I recoiled. "You haven't caught him yet?"

"This is an island. He's not going anywhere without us knowing." He puffed up his chest.

His assurance didn't fill me with confidence. "Are we done here? I have to get home."

I didn't wait for an answer before I wrestled on my backpack and left. My mind reeled like I was hearing of Dad's accident for the first time again, but now, it was much worse. And they hadn't even caught the guy. What if he planned to return and finish the job?

CHAPTER FOUR

My thighs burned by the time I crested the hill to my childhood home. Most of Sleeping Beauty Mountain still loomed high above me, the curve of her hip arching from east to west, lush with ancient trees. We lived on Elbow Hill, which presented a breathtaking view of the harbor and the strait beyond that. However, I was too anxious to speak with Dad to enjoy the scenery.

When I reached the two-story Victorian house near the end of the road, I threw open the wrought iron gate and shut it behind me. Nolan walked right through it, and the little black cat slipped between the pickets. I didn't shoo them away, mostly because I didn't think it would work.

Maybe my fiancé was following out of concern for me or Dad. Or else he still had the urge to haunt me. Yeah, because that was what I needed right now.

Once I'd raced across the pathway, I took the porch steps two at a time, automatically avoiding the third one—a habit formed during my teen years while dodging the creaky stair after curfew. I strode across the porch to the red front door and grasped the handle, ready to barge in. After all, Dad was expecting me, and this was my home. Or was it?

I froze. While I'd lived nowhere else over the years, except for my travel accommodations throughout Europe, it felt strange to be returning. And I didn't want to get too comfortable and risk slipping back into my old life. This was temporary.

In the end, I rapped on the door three times and burst in. It seemed like a fair compromise. Still following me, Nolan and my feline friend started forward.

"I'm sorry," I told them. "Now's not a good time."

I was looking at the cat, but I hoped they both understood. Though, judging by the disgruntled meow right before I closed the door, I doubted it.

Dropping my bag and jacket onto the worn hallway rug, I called out, "Dad?!"

A dish clattered in the kitchen, and footsteps approached. I knew once I saw him, I'd feel better. A moment later, he appeared at the other end of the hallway, but upon seeing him, I felt far from relieved.

My father's kind face was a patchwork quilt of purples and yellows, bruises in various stages of healing, and a sling held his casted right arm across his chest. The lines on his forehead appeared deeper, but at the sight of me, they relaxed.

I rushed down the hall and threw my arms around him. When he grunted, I tried to pull away, afraid I'd hurt him, but he only held me tighter.

"Welcome home, Vi."

"Some welcome." I drew back. "Look at you. Why didn't you tell me how bad it was?"

"I didn't want you to worry the entire trip back. It wouldn't have changed anything."

Throat tightening, I swallowed hard. Now, I understood why he'd avoided video chatting with me during my layover in Frankfurt.

When he bent to pick up my bag, I shot him a look and waved him toward the kitchen. We passed through the hallway lined with green hand-painted wallpaper and dark wainscoting. The house had changed very little since the first Woodses moved to the island and built it. There was probably a time it had felt dated, but now, it was something to be treasured. The nicked hardwood floors and tarnished brass doorknobs told a story of lives lived, keeping our lost family members close— you know, without living with a bunch of ghostly roommates.

Desperate for caffeine, I filled the kettle for tea. Dad limped toward the pedestal table tucked into the rounded nook that afforded a view of the garden. Not that there was much to admire this early in the year.

He groaned as he sat. "So, how was your flight?"

"Really? You're going to small talk me right now?" I turned on the stove and took a seat across from him. "I ran into Jason. He told me what happened." I wasn't about to get into the reason for our meeting yet.

Dad studied his good hand resting on the tabletop, knuckles puffed up like purple grapes. "I was working late when the thief broke in. Since I was in the bathroom, I didn't hear him until he started smashing display cases, dumping everything into a duffel bag." He shook his head. "Years of work. So much money lost. Pieces you sent back from Europe, and other… irreplaceable items."

I didn't ask what those were, because it didn't matter. Instead, I laid a hand over his. "Dad, the only thing irreplaceable is you."

He gave me a wan smile. "I just reacted. I grabbed the wrench from under the bathroom sink and chased him out. He took off, but something in me couldn't let him go. So I ran after him."

I pressed a palm to my forehead. "Tell me you didn't. This exact scenario is what insurance is for."

"I know. I wasn't thinking. Once I caught up to him, my brain caught up with me, and I stood there, not sure what to do next. He tackled me, and we grappled on the boardwalk.

Your old man got in a few hits." He grinned briefly. "Then he stomped on my ribs, cracking several, and broke my arm."

Emotions roiled inside me: hatred for the man who did this and frustration that the sheriff hadn't caught him. Hope City barely had five thousand people, so how hard could it be to track down one person? Finally, I landed on guilt. If only I'd been there, not gallivanting across Europe. If only I'd never left to begin with. If only…

"Dad, I'm so sorry."

He stared at me. "For what? You didn't do this. It was just some lowlife looking for a quick buck."

"If you hadn't been alone, then—"

"What? You would have chased him out with the broom? This is nobody's fault but that thug's. And I shouldn't have followed him. It felt so personal, though. The store has been in our family for six generations. It's a part of me. Of us." His hand clenched into a fist until he winced and let it relax. "I remember you helping around the place after school and coloring in the back room, your mom constantly tweaking and perfecting the display cases…"

He seemed to go somewhere else or, rather, sometime else. Back to when the three of us had been a family, before Mom left him with a seven-year-old daughter. Like always, I wanted to understand why she'd taken off. However, now wasn't the best time to ask about it, and he'd only avoid the subject like usual.

Dad inhaled deeply, as though waking from a dream. "Anyway, thank you for coming home. I couldn't have run the store alone. The pain medication makes me loopy. About a dozen times a day, I walk into a room and can't remember why I'm there."

I snorted. "That's not unusual."

"True. But now, I have an excuse."

A high-pitched whistle filled the room, and I pulled the kettle off the stove. While we still had a lot to discuss, I needed to be more focused to continue, so I pressed pause for now and grabbed a mug.

"There's some chai in the cupboard," my dad said. "I had Mrs. Freeman buy some for you."

I nearly dropped the mug. "Mrs. Freeman? Has there been a ceasefire? You two haven't been on the best of terms since her vervain started creeping into our vegetable garden."

Dad sniffed. "They nearly snuffed out our tomatoes last year. The darn things are a weed, and she insists on planting them so close to the fence."

Something told me the ceasefire with our neighbor would be temporary.

I found the new tea canister and popped open the top, inhaling deeply before scooping out the dried mix. The cuckoo clock on the wall struck ten a.m., and the enthusiastic bird darted in and out. I'd always found the thing annoying. Now, it seemed to say, "Welcome home. Welcome home. Welcome home."

Surrounded by all this familiarity, it felt as though I'd never left, like my absence had changed nothing. That was reinforced when my fiancé strolled into the kitchen, unbuttoned his suit jacket, and took a seat next to my father.

While it's not like I'd thought a closed door would stop a ghost, I'd hoped manners would. I gritted my teeth but kept my expression neutral. My dad had enough to worry about without learning of my curse.

As the two of them sat in comfortable silence, it took me back to a better time, and a lump formed in my throat. I'd had five years to accept Nolan's death, to find closure. However, the ache behind my ribcage told me my time abroad had only set it aside. Like I'd walked out of an untidy kitchen, hoping that when I returned, it would have cleaned itself.

After plopping the tea steeper in, I poured the water into my mug and looked up. Dad and Nolan were watching me, the same wistful expression on their faces. It was unnerving.

I forced a smile. "What?"

"It's good to have you home, Vi," Dad said.

I wished I could say I was happy to be home. "It's good to see you too."

The doorbell's cheerful chime filled the house, and I reluctantly left my steeping caffeine to answer it. Jason was standing on the porch, and he wasn't alone. Next to him, Sheriff Reed removed his hat and stepped forward, gold star gleaming on his chest.

The gray that used to fleck his temples now covered the rest of his head. His mustache hung limp above his upper lip, and his face appeared drawn like he'd lost too much weight. The man's appearance brought to mind the weather-beaten boardwalk in the older sections of downtown.

Reed regarded me with frosty blue eyes. "You're back." He sounded disgruntled rather than surprised. Of course, Jason would have filled him in.

Why did I keep having to defend my return? "Last time I checked, Sheriff, this was my home."

He stepped closer, like he might walk right in. "Is your father here? I need to speak with him."

"He's not feeling well. In case you haven't heard, he was attacked. Apparently, the crook responsible is still on the loose." I layered my tone with an extra serving of judgment.

"Not anymore," he said.

Dad shuffled out of the kitchen and down the hall to join us. "Does that mean you've caught him?"

"In a way," the sheriff said, drawing out the words. "The body of the offender, Wyatt Thorn, was found floating in the ferry slip this morning. By your daughter, actually. I was hoping to ask you a few questions." The tone of his gravelly voice made it clear he wasn't hoping so much as demanding.

My dad shot me a curious look but stepped aside. "I guess you'd better come in."

CHAPTER FIVE

I'd hoped to avoid many people on my first day back, dead and alive. So far, I'd been lucky enough to run into most of them. However, if I had to choose one person I could have done without, it was Sheriff Reed. And now, he was standing in my living room.

"Is this going to take long?" I asked him. "My dad needs his rest."

The sheriff eyed me, probably debating if he should kick me out now. "Not long. Since the deceased was the one who broke into Charming Treasures, I wanted to tie up loose ends now that we've... got the guy."

No thanks to his amazing detective skills.

Dad eased himself into his favorite leather recliner by the fireplace and invited the two men to sit. Unfortunately, Jason chose the spot on the couch Nolan had always preferred in life —and death, apparently, because he was already sitting there. He leaped to his semitransparent feet, narrowly missing Jason's butt.

I wondered if it would have hurt Nolan or felt uncomfortable. Physically speaking, of course. Socially speaking, being someone's chair would be uncomfortable for anyone, living or dead.

Scowling at the deputy, he went to stand by the large bay window. I didn't get how ghosts sat anyway. I wasn't a physics genius, but if they couldn't tread water, how did their backside meet resistance on the cushions?

Reed declined the offer to sit, standing like he had a ruler for a spine. I stood too. His presence didn't exactly fill me with warm, fuzzy feelings. Not when the last time we'd spoken, he'd accused me of having something to do with my fiancé's death. I mean, I blamed myself for it, but not in the way he suspected.

While he hadn't believed my story that someone had tampered with the vehicle, he'd homed in on me and my inexplicable survival, as though I'd lied about being in the car at all. Then, out of nowhere, he'd declared it a simple mechanical malfunction, case closed, despite my key witness statement to the contrary. The investigation had been bungled, and though I'd fought it as much as I could, between my heartache, Nolan haunting me, and the Abernathys turning on me, I'd been in no shape to pick up the ball Reed had dropped.

The sheriff took out a pen and notepad from his shirt pocket and faced my dad. "First, I want to review the list of items you reported stolen."

Dad shifted as though he couldn't get comfortable. "That was an educated guess. I can't be sure what's missing without checking the store's inventory."

Reed flipped back a few pages. "You seemed fairly certain about some items. Several engagement rings, a pocket watch, two tennis bracelets, a ruby necklace, and a set of emerald earrings with a matching pendant. Oh, and an art deco ring." He pronounced the last like the 1920s style was new to him.

Dad cleared his throat. "It was a set of rings. An engagement ring and wedding band." Their loss seemed to disturb him the most.

I drew in a sharp breath. "The family rings?"

He grimaced. "Yes. I brought them to the shop to clean

them that night. They were sitting on my work table, making them easy to grab."

My great-great-grandfather had made the pair to propose to his wife. The engagement ring's diamond was a rare Asscher cut, and smaller diamonds formed a dazzling geometric puzzle around it. I'd always dreamed of wearing them one day. So those were the other "irreplaceable items" Dad had meant.

I turned to the sheriff. "Have you found any of the missing jewelry yet?"

"We've recovered a couple of pieces. Not the art deco rings, I'm afraid." He refocused his attention on my dad. "Stanley, can you tell me your whereabouts last night?"

My brain jolted to attention at the question. Frowning, I tried to catch Jason's eye. He was busy scribbling in his own notebook. No doodles. They must have meant business.

Dad gestured around us. "I was here, watching TV. Mrs. Freeman dropped off a lasagna and some groceries at about six-thirty. Other than that, I was here alone."

Reed made a note. "Do you have something to confirm that? A security system, a doorbell camera, anything?"

"No. I've never felt the need for one." Absently, he rubbed his cast. "Until now, that is."

My frown deepened. The break-and-enter investigation was technically solved. And if the sheriff was there to tie up those loose ends, there was no need for an alibi. That could only mean one thing.

I stepped between the two men. "Do you think my dad had something to do with the thief's death?"

Reed's world-weary features remained stiff and unreadable. "We're only asking questions."

"But you suspect it was a murder?" Of course, I already knew Wyatt Thorn had been strangled, thanks to Jason's slipup. However, I didn't want to get him in trouble.

"I'm not at liberty to share any details yet," the sheriff said robotically.

"You heard my dad. He was here all night."

His attention flicked to my father as though watching for a reaction. "Except that we have an eyewitness who says they saw him on the promenade last night."

My dad's head jerked. "Oh… that's right. I'm sorry. I've been absentminded ever since the incident." He chuckled, rubbing his bald spot. "I was restless, so I walked down to the store around nine to tidy up the place. It wasn't long before the pain kicked in, and I returned home."

Without a reply, the sheriff jotted down this new revelation. I could only imagine what he was writing. I wanted to slap my forehead. Of all the important facts for Dad to forget, it had to be one that made him look guiltier for not mentioning it.

"He's on pain medication," I said defensively. "He told me it's been causing forgetfulness."

Sheriff Reed ran a knuckle across his chin as he regarded me. "Is that so? Have you noticed any other changes in your dad's behavior?"

The unspoken question was loud and clear: like any violent tendencies?

"My dad isn't a murderer. Besides, why would he take the law into his own hands when we have such capable law enforcement in town?" I coated each word with sarcasm.

Jason looked up from his notes. "Hey! What did I do?"

I ignored him. "And remember, we have insurance to cover theft, so what would his motive be?"

Reed's mustache twitched, hinting at a self-satisfied smile. "Money can't replace everything, as you demonstrated with your reaction to the news about your family's rings. Maybe he wanted them back. Or it might have been for revenge."

I flung an arm in my dad's direction. "Does it look like he's in any condition to kill someone? How would he overpower a man who sent him to the hospital in the first place?"

"He could have asked someone else for help. Or perhaps he caught Wyatt off guard. The coroner's report won't be back for another few days. For now, I'm just getting a jump on the case. So if you're done interfering, why don't you let the investigator do the actual investigating?"

"I wasn't aware one would be joining us. Will he be here soon?" I peered out the window, pretending to search for somebody, anybody, more capable than the sheriff. All I saw was the black cat pacing near the vervain sprouting from the ground on our side of the fence. "Because the last time I checked, your track record isn't so good."

My dig at the sheriff's competency finally cracked his cool facade, and he took a step closer to me. He wasn't a tall man. We stood eye to eye, but the fact that he had the power to arrest me still gave him intimidation points.

"Miss Woods, I'll have to ask you to wait outside." He made eye contact with Jason and tilted his head toward me in a silent exchange.

The deputy jumped to his feet and placed a hand on my arm to escort me out. Scowling, I flicked it away.

He showed me his palms in surrender. "Vi, please. Don't make this any harder than it needs to be."

"Too late," I said. "The sheriff is already involved."

And like a bouncer kicking out a disruptive drunk, he ushered me out of my house. Some welcome home.

CHAPTER SIX

The moment I stepped outside, I began to pace across my front lawn. Now and then, I peeked through the living room window to spy on Dad and the sheriff. The black cat sat on the porch, observing me through her half-lidded eyes. I swore she was judging me.

My gaze flitted over the property. Nolan might have been watching me, too, but the clouds had dispersed, and the midday sun shone brightly. In this light, he'd appear as a mere shimmer in the air, and I was too tired to play I Spy right now.

The front door opened, and Jason came out to join me. "Violet, talk to me."

"You already took my statement at the ferry terminal, remember?"

"I don't mean as a deputy." He descended the stairs to block my pacing. "Talk to me as a friend."

I huffed. "We both know my dad wouldn't hurt a fly."

He toed the grass with his boot. "According to his own statement, he chased after Wyatt with a wrench, and I don't think it was to fix his leaky sink."

Okay, he had a point, but I wasn't about to give in. "Dad was like a dog chasing after a bus. Once he caught up, he had no idea what he'd planned to do, as you can see by the state of him."

Jason looked as though he wanted to agree with me, but the badge on his chest prevented him from doing so. "Sometimes, investigations are the process of eliminating names off a list. So sit back and let us eliminate your dad's name." He rested his hand on my shoulder. "I'm sure everything will turn out all right."

His palm felt warm and reassuring. The uniform he wore felt less so. However, I had to admit it was nice to have a friend not only on my side but in the sheriff's ear.

The cedar hedge next to us rustled, startling me, and I peered over at Mrs. Freeman's place. Her silver locks, neatly wound in the shape of a beehive, bobbed above the greenery. It was as if the avid gardener wanted to tempt the pollinators to her early bloomers.

"Good morning, Mrs. Freeman," I called out.

Even at twenty-seven, I couldn't bring myself to use her first name. The whole town had either known her as a teacher or, like Jason and me, an elementary school principal. Then, when I was seven, she moved in next door, becoming my neighbor: every kid's dream come true. All of Hope still called her Mrs. Freeman; she didn't exactly put off a first-name-basis vibe.

"Is that Violet I hear?" Her clipped voice cut through the evergreen foliage.

I followed her tower of hair down the length of the hedges that lined the wrought iron fence until we came to a gap. The older woman stood a few inches shorter than me in her floral ensemble, from a shirt embroidered with roses to a cheerful pair of sunflower boots. A woven basket of trimmings and weeds hung from her arm. I swore she was an immortal who never aged, or rather, who remained the same old age.

She took me in from head to toe. "It is you. Your father said you'd be home soon."

My stalker cat leaped onto the fence, tiptoeing between the finial-topped pickets.

Mrs. Freeman nodded to the animal. "Good day," she said in a way she might greet a colleague.

The feline dipped her head and meowed. I swore it could have been an actual response, but she probably wanted a scratch under the chin. When she didn't receive one, she resumed her balancing act toward the backyard.

I shook off the weird exchange and turned back to my neighbor. "I arrived this morning. Thank you for looking out for my dad. He said you brought over your famous lasagna and picked up groceries."

"It was no problem," she said as though anyone would do it. "He's in quite rough shape. I hope they find the good-for-nothing who did this to him. I've never seen him so mad at anyone in all the years I've known him. And that's a long time. I taught him when he was a boy."

Like I said, immortal.

I flashed a look at Jason, who stood back, hidden from Mrs. Freeman's sight. "Well, he seems in good spirits now," I said dismissively.

She continued, too focused on snipping an errant twig with her shears. "It wasn't the injuries that made him so mad. It was the thieving. I once had my purse snatched in broad daylight. Something like that makes you feel violated. Even years later, I wanted to get my hands on the hooligan, so I can sympathize with your dad's desire."

Grass swished behind me as Jason joined us. I cringed.

He took out the notepad from his shirt pocket. "You mean Mr. Woods said something about wanting to go after the thief?"

Mrs. Freeman jumped at his appearance, a wrinkle forming on her brow. "Oh… sure. What was it he said? Something like 'If I ever get my hands on him…'" Her narrowed eyes scanned Jason's uniform. "What brings you here, boy?"

As though to prove he wasn't a boy anymore, he straightened his posture, standing a little taller. Not that he wasn't tall enough already. "Official business."

The woman sniffed. "Now, you listen to me, Jason Swan. I've known you since before you could tie your own laces, and I remember giving you detention for putting slugs in the girls' shoes. So don't you 'official business' me, young man."

He ducked his blond head, and I snickered. As her sharp gaze landed on me, I stifled my laughter. She had more than a few embarrassing stories from my childhood.

"Deputy Swan's here because the man who robbed my father was murdered last night." I widened my eyes in case she needed a bigger hint.

The older woman held a gloved hand to her mouth, brushing dirt onto her upper lip like a mustache. "Oh, dear. That's unfortunate. But surely, Stanley had nothing to do with that."

Jason consulted his notes. "You stated you heard him say, and I quote, 'If I ever get my hands on him…' What was the rest of that sentence, Mrs. Freeman?"

"Th-That doesn't mean anything. People say all kinds of things during times of stress." Clutching her basket close, she backed away. "I just remembered, I left the kettle on inside. Violet, it's so nice to have you back."

She turned on her rubber boots and all but raced inside her home. It was easy to guess who the sheriff would visit next.

When I faced Jason, he pressed his lips together with a look that said *I told you so*.

I planted my fists on my hips. "You heard what she said. Who wouldn't be spouting threats after what Wyatt Thorn did? Don't you remember the time Lucy Litton told everyone I still wet the bed in tenth grade? I threatened to shave her hair off, but I never really would have done anything." I was still tempted to, though, even after all these years.

"Yes," he agreed. "But Lucy didn't turn up dead shortly

after. We can't ignore the uttered threats about a man who was just murdered."

While I knew he was right, I wouldn't admit it if my life depended on it.

The front door squeaked open, and the sheriff exited the house. He donned his hat and tipped it in farewell to my dad before crossing the yard.

I scowled as he neared. "Finished interrogating an injured man?"

"Just following the clues."

His dismissiveness irritated me more. "You didn't follow the clues after my fiancé's death. That case still on your back burner?"

"I've got a few new ideas." He squared off with me. "And now that you're back in town, we should have a chat at the station sometime."

I flinched. "What's that supposed to mean?"

Reed gave no response. Something told me he didn't mean for us to partner up and solve the cold case together.

Could he still suspect I had something to do with Nolan's death, even after he'd declared it an accident? Maybe it was the giant chunks missing from my story that still bothered him. It wasn't like I could have told him what really happened that night, the heavy confession my fiancé had dropped on me: that he was a supposed warlock. Even I still had a hard time believing it and had all but explained it away over the years.

"So is that why you're harassing my dad?" I asked. "Because you've got a problem with me?"

"No. I'm here because I'm a good detective." He ignored my snort. "I may not have been able to solve Nolan's case, but you can be certain I'll solve this one." It sounded more like a threat than a promise. "Oh, and your dad said you'd get me the shop's inventory list. Be sure to hand it over ASAP."

I gave him a saccharine smile. "I'll put a rush order on it for you."

"Need a ride downtown?" he asked.

I'm sure he would have loved taking a mental picture of me in the back of his patrol vehicle. "I'm fine, thanks."

But he must have predicted the answer because he was already opening the driver's door to slip behind the wheel. Jason joined him, giving me an awkward wave goodbye.

Dad came to stand by me, more than likely to stop me from doing anything foolish. What was I going to do, toilet paper the sheriff's SUV? I wasn't sixteen anymore.

As we watched them drive away, I dwelled on the sheriff's words, on the phrasing he'd used. *I may not have been able to solve Nolan's case.* He hadn't said he couldn't. He'd said he wasn't able to. What had changed so that he was able to now? My return? Maybe I didn't want him digging into that cold case after all. I'd been on that roller coaster before, and it had taken me for a ride and spat me right off the island. I wasn't eager for round two.

Dad wrapped an arm around me. "Don't worry. It will all work out."

I wished I shared his confidence in the sheriff's abilities, but I'd already watched him botch one investigation. If I wanted to ensure my dad didn't end up in jail, I needed to give Reed a nudge in a different direction.

CHAPTER SEVEN

Charming Treasures.

I stood beneath the sign that had been hand painted and repaired by several Woods generations and peered through the multipaned window. It was too dark to see anything. Normally, our family shop, a place filled with precious memories and endless inspiration, would have been calling to me. Now, I feared what waited inside. There was no time to waste, however, since I had a lot of work to do if I was going to help clear my dad's name.

Sticking the key into the lock, I noted the plywood covering a broken window pane. Wyatt Thorn's entry point. When I swung open the door, the familiar scent of wood polish and window cleaner surrounded me.

I stepped inside, and something crunched under my shoe: shattered glass from the surrounding cases that lay half empty. As the midday light poured in, the hardwood floor sparkled like diamonds had been scattered across it. More glass.

My hands automatically clenched. I understood my father's outrage, the violation Mrs. Freeman had mentioned, and I wasn't even the one with a broken arm. I didn't blame him for taking action. If I'd been there that night, I would have chased the thief too. But I hadn't been there. Unable to cope with the aftermath of the car accident, I'd left my dad all alone.

Well, I was here now, and I was going to do everything I could to help set things right.

I slipped into the back, turned on the radio for some noise, and grabbed a broom. As I tidied, I considered my first step. While I feared for my dad's future, reputation, and mental health, I couldn't let my emotions get the best of me. I had to stay calm and rational, be Miss Levelheaded, if I was going to be useful.

The sheriff had said they'd only recovered a couple of items. Either Wyatt had hidden the jewelry well or he'd already sold it all, which seemed unlikely since there'd been little time between the burglary and his death. A third possibility, and the one I was counting on, was that whoever killed him had taken the rest. If I could find that jewelry, I might be one step closer to finding the murderer.

After confirming which pieces were missing, I'd search every pawn shop, consignment store, and boutique on the island to see if any had turned up—hey, no one ever accused criminals of being geniuses. Any business would have records of who dropped off the jewelry, giving the sheriff a new lead.

As I dwelled on his unwelcome visit, my earlier irritation returned, and I swept up the glass with more gusto than neces- sary. If he'd thought I'd had something to do with Nolan's death, then why hadn't he pursued it further at the time? Why let me leave Charm Island?

I'd mentally replayed the night of the accident so many times, starting with the awful rehearsal dinner and my argu- ment with Nolan's pretentious father and mother. I was to marry their son the next morning, and they'd chosen that moment, in front of all our family and friends, to beg Nolan to reconsider his decision.

Disgusted at them, at my fiancé for not standing up for us, I stormed outside. Nolan followed me, pleading with me to come back. When I refused, he asked the question weighing on both our minds.

"Do you still want to get married tomorrow?"

I loved Nolan. But while both he and his kid sister were as sweet as could be, his parents were unbearable. Did I want to be tied to them forever?

Still, I said yes.

He didn't look relieved. Avoiding my gaze, he kicked a rock with a shoe that cost more than all of mine combined. "First, there's something you should know. Something I should have told you a long time ago."

I licked my dry lips. "What is it?"

"I'm…" His face twisted like it was physically painful to get the words out. "A warlock."

I snickered. Typical Nolan, always trying to lighten the mood. "What? As in a wizard or whatever?"

But he wasn't laughing. "Don't freak out, okay?"

Which was exactly what people said before they freaked you out.

Producing his pocket knife, he released the blade. He raised it in the air before unceremoniously stabbing it into his palm.

With a cry, I lurched to grab his wrist. However, the point never punctured his skin. It bounced off like he or the knife were made of rubber. Of course, it was just a trick. Nolan loved his little pranks.

"That's not funny." I grabbed for the fake knife.

"Vi, wait—"

Pain lanced across my palm, and I dropped the blade. Blood welled on my skin. I'd been cut.

My breaths coming faster, I stared at Nolan, less concerned about my injury than the reality sinking in. "But… how?"

He reached for my hand and placed his over mine. It was a strange thing to do. The wound was stitch-worthy, and I needed a compress, not comfort.

After a few seconds, my skin tingled with warmth, like I

was holding it too close to a fire. When he pulled away, the gash had vanished. Only the spilled blood remained smeared across my skin.

A laugh slipped out of me. Not a humorous one but panicked. Concern creased Nolan's handsome face, and he reached for me again. I recoiled.

I. Lost. It. I left Miss Levelheaded in the dust as I ran for my life.

If I'd stopped to think it through, been rational about it, I would have remembered I'd been with Nolan since junior year. He didn't tell me his secret so he could use some sort of hex on me after all this time.

But I didn't think. I operated on pure fear until I ran smack dab into Sheriff Reed, wide-eyed, crying, and covered in my blood.

The older man's hand automatically brushed his gun holster. I probably looked wild or guilty of something.

He gripped my arms and locked gazes with me. "What's wrong? Are you okay?"

What was I supposed to say, that my fiancé was a warlock? The sheriff would have organized a manhunt with pitchforks and torches or else thrown me into a padded room. Besides, I didn't even know what it all meant yet.

Maybe Nolan had joined a strange cult who called themselves warlocks, or he was practicing to become a magician—and if so, bonus points for a realistic illusion. While my raw nerves told me that wasn't it, my brain kept searching for a plausible explanation.

I mumbled an excuse to the sheriff and got out of there as fast as I could. I couldn't trust him with Nolan's secret, but I didn't trust Nolan right then either. So I ran to the place I felt safest. To Max.

When Nolan finally tracked me down, I'd calmed enough to go for a drive with him and talk. He begged me to keep his secret. While he wasn't the man I thought I knew, I was still me, and betraying him didn't feel right. I also needed time to ask questions and understand everything. What he was expecting me to believe didn't just change how I saw us. It changed my whole world. That wasn't something you came to terms with in a single night, especially the night before your wedding.

"Don't worry," I told him. "I'll take it to my grave."

If only I knew how close I was about to come to it.

Moments later, Nolan lost control of the car. Or more like the car had taken control, giving the steering wheel a mind of its own. When he took his foot off the gas and hit the useless brake, the engine revved, accelerating us toward a hairpin turn. We blasted through the barrier, hurtling over the cliffs and plunging into the deep bay below.

I blacked out. When I came to, it was cold, dark. My head throbbed, and my vision swam.

This is it, I thought.

Groping around, I found Nolan's hand. It was limp.

Water was filling the car. Panic. Helplessness. Then my window broke. No more air.

Later, when I woke in the hospital, I had no idea how I'd survived. Nolan stood near the foot of my bed. At the sight of him, a euphoric surge of relief hit me. Everything was going to be okay.

Of course, everything wasn't okay. He'd died in that accident, and while we'd never walk down the aisle, I'd be tied to him for eternity if I didn't escape the island.

When the sheriff asked about our run-in that night, I pretended I couldn't remember it. It seemed the safest thing to do. But it only added to his doubts about how I'd survived and gotten to shore. Even I didn't have an answer for that one. It was impossible.

After I left the island, I wondered if I'd imagined everything, if the stress and trauma had altered my memory of that night's events. Magic couldn't be real. On the other hand, I now saw dead people, so maybe warlocks weren't so far-fetched. Though I preferred to avoid that line of thinking because it seemed to have no end. If warlocks were real, then there was a chance other beings were real, too, and I couldn't even handle ghosts.

In the end, I found it hard to resent my curse. It felt like a much-deserved punishment. If I hadn't overreacted to Nolan's confession, had remained levelheaded, we could have talked things out. He wouldn't have had to drive all over town to look for me, and he might still be alive. We'd probably be married, I wouldn't be cursed, and the Abernathys wouldn't hate me and my dad. Well, not as much.

Now, Dad needed me—the levelheaded me—to help him. I wouldn't let my emotions get the best of me again.

I swept the last speck of glass into a dustpan and dumped it in the trash. When I spun back around, from the corner of my eye, I spotted a figure across the room. A man was in the store with me!

A strangled yelp caught in my chest, and I gripped the broom like a weapon. He didn't notice. His intense gaze was locked on something inside one of the cases.

Right. It was a shop. With so much talk of thieves and murderers, I'd forgotten people might want to come in for less nefarious reasons than cleaning us out.

I glanced at the front door. I'd forgotten to lock it behind me. However, our sign remained flipped to Closed, and the lights were off since enough daylight streamed through the windows. And if that hadn't been enough, you'd think the guy would have questioned all the broken cases.

Killing the music, I cleared my throat. "I'm sorry. I didn't hear you come in."

No response. Did he think I was talking to someone else? The man struck me as familiar, but from where?

I tried again. "We're not open today. You'll have to come back."

His head twitched in my direction, but he otherwise ignored me, his attention never straying from the case.

My skin prickled as my suspicions rose again. While Wyatt Thorn was dead, there could have been two people in on the robbery. Maybe his partner in crime had returned to finish the job.

Clutching my broom, I sidled toward the exit. When the man was caught between me and the window, the daylight shone right through his body.

He was a ghost. I finally placed him. Of all the spirits I had to run into today, why him?

"Wyatt?" I gritted my teeth. "You've got some nerve coming back here."

As he practically drooled over our merchandise, I realized why he'd be drawn to our store. Robbing us had been one of his final tasks in life, one that was interrupted. Perhaps his desire to clean out the rest of the store was keeping him trapped on our plane of existence. Well, not on my watch.

I raised my broom high and swung it at his head. It sailed right through, but he flinched out of human habit. Next, I dragged out the vacuum and tried to suck him up. Obviously, it didn't work. It made me feel a little better, though.

With a sigh, I gave up and turned my back on him. I hated that he was hanging around, but I needed to keep working if I was going to search for the stolen jewelry. Thankfully, I had a lot of practice ignoring the dead.

I rounded the end of the display case and booted up the shop's old computer. It whirred to life, and I crossed my fingers it wouldn't choose this moment to kick the bucket. Back when I'd first graduated from business school, I'd set up a digital filing system to keep track of everything coming and going from the store. Unfortunately, a quick browse through the saved documents revealed Dad hadn't used it since I'd left.

Groaning, I pulled out a behemoth binder from under the counter and opened it up. Sure enough, he'd reverted to our super high-tech filing system: a photo of each piece of jewelry taped to a page of handwritten notes. I'd tried many times to usher Dad into the twenty-first century, but he was stuck in his ways.

Binder in hand, I went around the store and, one by one, checked off the remaining jewelry until the only display case left was the one Wyatt stood by. As I approached, he moved aside, either as a knee-jerk reaction or because he sensed I needed space—both physically and emotionally.

He hadn't been a bad-looking guy. There was a rogue charm about him, his full lips poised between a devilish grin and a secretive smirk. I imagined his brown eyes usually flashed with mischievousness, but right now, the semitransparent skin around them was tense with anxiety.

Was the mystery of his murder keeping him from moving on to wherever spirits went? Instead of window shopping for all the jewelry he hadn't stolen, he should have been lurking around his killer.

The moment I slid the case open, he moved closer to peer over my shoulder. The hair on the back of my neck rose as though I felt him breathing down it.

"You know you can't take them with you, right?" I snapped.

Rolling my shoulders, I returned my attention to the binder. As I sorted through the pieces, I discovered one that wasn't in the book: a three-stone emerald necklace.

Diligently, I flipped through the pages again, but there was no record of it. Could Dad have forgotten to document it? It seemed unlikely; he was meticulous.

To have a closer peek at the necklace, I reached into the case. The moment my fingers grazed it, I recoiled.

Three perfect princess-cut gems had been half swallowed by poorly soldered yellow gold. They didn't line up evenly, and the claws holding them in place stuck out like thorns. It was worse than my first attempt when Dad had handed me a torch at thirteen.

But it was more than the shoddy craftsmanship that sent my sixth sense humming. They *felt* wrong.

A few weeks after the car accident, I'd learned my strange connection to the spirit world somehow extended to jewelry. It was as if anyone who wore a piece left an ethereal fingerprint on it, allowing me glimpses into their thoughts and memories. The longer they'd worn it or the stronger the personality, the easier it was for me to read them and estimate the value of the pieces. It was the one thing my curse was actually good for: seeking diamonds in the rough.

Once I'd discovered the ability, I started sending items back to Charming Treasures or sold them to finance my travels. There was a reason I hadn't needed to work a normal job in five years.

Combing through the binder again, I found an entry for an emerald earring and necklace set I'd purchased in France, the same set my father had confirmed stolen earlier that day. I compared the detailed notes, and my sixth sense, to the gemstones in the mangled pendant.

They were the same ones.

A sick realization slid over me. While the pendant resembled a child's first attempt at jewelry making, it also could have been created by someone with their dominant arm in a cast. Was that what Dad had been doing here late the night before? Not cleaning up, like he'd claimed, but trying to conceal the "stolen" emeralds in this train wreck of a setting?

When I turned to Wyatt, his glare sent a jolt racing to my toes. It struck me as accusatory or conspiratorial. Was he haunting his murderer after all?

I didn't want to believe it. Couldn't believe it. Yet here was the evidence literally on display. Had my father killed him?

There was only one person who could tell me that now.

CHAPTER EIGHT

Upon returning home with the emerald necklace, I discovered my new cat friend waiting for me on the porch. The moment I opened the door, she darted through my legs and into the house. I didn't stop her. I was on a mission.

Dad was snoring in his chair with a book on his lap. He'd obviously been that way for some time, because the sun had long since set, and the room was dark but for the moonlight streaming through the window. Nolan occupied his usual spot on the sofa, one leg crossed over the other, an argyle sock peeking out. In the dim light, he appeared all too real.

After my run-in with Wyatt, Nolan's calm appearance was a stark contrast. He seemed to have a better grasp on the whole afterlife thing, maintaining his demeanor and quirks from when he'd been alive. While that hadn't been the case after he'd first died, perhaps time had allowed him to get a better grip on reality.

As I crossed the room, he followed my progress with his keen eyes. Shivering beneath his stare, I reached for the Tiffany lamp next to him so he'd appear less solid.

Click.

My dad snorted himself awake and sat the chair upright.

"Oh, Vi. I was just—" He jumped as the cat leaped onto his lap. "Hello there. Where did you come from?"

I shrugged. "She followed me home earlier."

That seemed a good enough answer for him, and he petted the little home invader. "How did things go at the store?"

Without another word, I held up the botched emerald necklace. He grew pale and shrank in on himself, gaze boring into the area rug.

I guessed that confirmed they were the so-called stolen emeralds. Hopefully, he'd reclaimed them only after Wyatt was killed by someone else. While swiping jewelry off a dead man wasn't ideal, it was better than being a murderer.

"Dad, did you have something to do with Wyatt Thorn's death?"

He pushed down the chair's footrest and scrubbed a hand over his face. "Of course not. How could you think that?"

Relieved, I sank onto the sofa, leaving space between me and Nolan. I knew Dad couldn't have killed someone, but a part of me was comforted to hear the denial from his own lips. "Then how did you get these jewels back?"

He heaved a sigh. "During our wrestling match, some jewelry dropped out of his duffel bag and slipped through a gap in the boardwalk. Afterward, while I was lying there, I saw they hadn't fallen into the water. So once the doctor released me from the hospital, I climbed down along the rocks next to our store and got them."

I pictured him navigating the slick cliff face in the dark with a broken arm, one wrong move away from plunging into the marina. Or worse, onto the rocks. "In your condition? Dad, you could have died." It didn't seem worth it. There was a piece of the story missing.

He raised his shoulders in a helpless gesture then winced and massaged the injured one. Unsympathetic to his pain, his furry companion wedged her head beneath his hand in a not-so-subtle hint.

My temples throbbed. I dropped the necklace onto the coffee table, and the pressure behind my eyeballs eased. However, the spirits connected to the gems still called to me, voicing their outrage at what had been done. "Dad, the man who supposedly stole these jewels wound up dead, and now you have them back in your possession? Do you have any idea how this looks?"

"At the time, he wasn't dead," he said weakly.

"Why would you even risk it? Why remake them instead of telling the sheriff you got them back?" But I already had an idea.

Closing his eyes, he took a moment to answer. "To claim the insurance money and still resell them without drawing attention." He gestured to the necklace. "This wasn't the only one I planned to alter. There are a few others locked in the shop's safe." His voice grew so quiet I could barely hear him over the contented purr coming from his lap.

That explained his discomfort during the sheriff's visit. He'd been lying.

"Insurance fraud? This isn't like you."

He fixed his gaze on the cat. "I can't say I was in the right frame of mind, especially once they gave me pain medication. My thoughts kept going around in circles. I added up all the bills, the lost time and work, taxes, and I knew the store wouldn't survive it. Business hasn't been good. Not since… the accident."

Nolan shifted uncomfortably, mouth set in a grim line as he stared at the sofa cushion. Did he understand what we were saying? Was he aware of the trouble his parents had caused us?

If I'd expected the tragedy to bring the Abernathys and me closer, I'd been way off base. In their grief and anger, they'd wanted someone to blame, and I fit the bill. They boycotted our store and turned half the town against us. The mainland jewelry shops started getting all our business.

We'd nearly been family, so I'd wanted to confront them

and reason with them, but I hesitated. Ever since Nolan's confession, my unanswered questions had been building. Was what he'd shown me even real? If magic existed, maybe that meant Quinton Abernathy had powers, too, a thought that kept me awake at night.

Even without magic, the mayor was the most powerful man on the island, and I'd made an enemy of him. So I used the money Nolan and I had saved for our honeymoon to buy a one-way ticket out of here. I'd hoped that if I left, the Abernathys would back off and things would improve for Dad. That didn't seem to be the case.

"This is all my fault," I said.

Dad leaned forward to rest a hand on my knee. "The Abernathys were wrong to act the way they did. That accident was in no way your fault. You almost died too."

Only I didn't die, and I couldn't resent them for despising me for it. I despised myself.

"And while the mayor has made a lot of trouble for the store—extra taxes, bogus permits, random safety inspections— I can't blame all my failures on them. The store has never been particularly successful under my care. The creative gene skipped me. You were always the artist, just like your grandfather."

Embarrassed, I rolled my eyes. "You taught me everything I know."

"I mean it. I might make quality pieces, but my strength lies in the tried-and-true staples. Wedding rings, diamond earrings, and keychain engravings." He sneered at the last one. "But we rely on tourists, and they don't buy staples. They want something special that reminds them of their holiday, and your original designs always caught their eye. What you can do with metal and jewels is nothing short of magic."

I wanted to dismiss everything he was saying. However, I'd always gotten the impression that if he hadn't felt obligated to carry on the family business, he might have been an accountant or something.

Dad slumped against his backrest like the confession had zapped his energy. "Anyway, things went downhill after you left. Eventually, I let go of my part-timer. I was barely keeping the lights on, then this happened." He gestured to his cast. "The shop wouldn't have survived until the insurance money came in, and I was desperate. Imagine, six generations of Woodses, and the store was going to die because of me."

Considering how good he was with numbers and balancing the books, I didn't doubt things were as dire as he made them out to be. "I had no idea. I'm so sorry."

With a throaty sound, he waved it off. "This is exactly why I didn't want to tell you. The store is my responsibility, not yours. You did what you needed to do. After everything that happened, I was relieved you were out there finding some peace."

My stomach twisted. Was that what I'd been doing? Because now that I was back, it was like nothing had changed. Worse yet, my absence had put a strain on Dad and the business. If not for me, he wouldn't have been driven to such extremes.

He picked up the emerald necklace from the table and ran a thumb over the jewels. The black cat touched its nose to it then leaped off his lap like it smelled something rotten.

"Your grandfather's probably rolling in his grave," he said. "The second I finished resetting the emeralds, I regretted it. I knew I couldn't go through with the insurance fraud scheme."

Despite the heavy situation or maybe because of it, a laugh bubbled out of me. "Because no one would buy the redesigns?"

A surprised snort escaped my dad, and he chuckled while clutching his side and wincing with each shake. "The necklace is pretty ugly, isn't it? In my defense, I was on a lot of painkillers." His smile faded, and the reprieve was over. "By the time I found my scruples again, I'd already shown the sheriff around the shop and given him a rundown of the missing jewels."

Unable to sit still any longer, I got to my feet and moved to the bay window. My hands twitched with the urge to draw the curtains as though we were having a clandestine meeting. Then again, I supposed we were.

My dad was in real trouble. If the necklace were to be discovered, it would elevate him to suspect number one if he wasn't already. Even Wyatt's ghost seemed to believe him guilty of foul play because of it. Maybe it wasn't enough evidence to send Dad to jail, but what if it went as far as court? How would we afford the lawyer, the downtime, the loss of reputation for the business? And I didn't even want to think about what the stress would do to his already compromised health.

"So what do we do now?" I asked him.

He slapped his thigh. "First thing tomorrow, I'll call the sheriff and fess up. It's not like I followed through with it. You can't go to jail for thinking of committing a crime."

Now I did shut the curtains. "I don't know. It would call your character into question, and in case you've forgotten, you're currently a suspect in a murder case."

Looking less certain, he rubbed his palm across his pant leg. "I'll tell them we found the emerald set in the shop. That I was confused from all the pain and medication, and I didn't have a good look at what Wyatt stole. Maybe I mixed up the jewelry."

I gestured to the necklace. "And if they discover your Frankensteined creation, you'll say what? That you were bored and decided to create a new setting? The sheriff's already on high alert. It will raise his suspicions of you."

Dad scratched his head absently. "Well, we can't dispose of the jewels."

"Definitely not."

His reasoning was likely about losing money in the long run. Mine was less logical. As a jeweler, it would break my heart. But more importantly, the spiritual connection I felt with the previously owned items and the souls who'd worn them in the past made it impossible. It would feel like throwing away a part of their essence. Once everything blew over, I wanted to see the pieces go to new homes, to gather more memories and touch more souls.

"Then we should temporarily hide the recovered jewelry," he said. "I didn't kill Wyatt Thorn. Once the sheriff comes to that conclusion, he'll move on to a new suspect. There'll be no need to lie about the jewels after that."

I didn't think it would be that easy. He was right about the recovered pieces, though. They needed to be hidden. For now.

My focus shifted to Nolan, who leaned forward on the sofa, elbows on knees, fingers steepled. I was more certain than ever that he was aware of everything. His expression seemed to say, *What on earth are you thinking?*

I was thinking that while messing with evidence was wrong, my dad going to jail for something he didn't do was even worse. I needed to escalate my investigation and hit the streets in the morning. It was no longer about finding a new suspect for the sheriff to focus on. If I was going to ensure my dad's freedom, I had to find the killer.

CHAPTER NINE

When I arrived at Charming Treasures first thing in the morning, there was no sign of Wyatt, and Nolan was off doing whatever ghosts did with all their free time. Hopefully, it would be a spirit-free day. After locking the door behind me, I headed into the back room and opened the old wall safe. A pile of hastily dumped jewelry stared back at me: the pieces Dad had retrieved from the cliffs at low tide.

Since our talk the night before, the shock had worn off, and reality was sinking in. I pinched the bridge of my nose. *Oh, Dad. Why did you do it?*

While I was tempted to dig a ten-foot-deep hole and dump all the recovered jewelry into it, I couldn't get rid of them. But where to hide the collection?

Call me paranoid, but I didn't want to walk out of the store with them. What if I was being watched—and not just by a ghost? I scanned the room, searching for a place to stash them. My gaze landed on the old hardwood floor.

Of course.

I raced to the back corner of the shop and sank to my knees. Sliding my hands over the wood planks, I found the right spot and pressed down. An entire section of the floor came away to reveal a hidden compartment lined with velvet.

It had been part of the shop's original build, the floorboards cut seamlessly so no one but a nosy child would ever find it. My dad never had a need for it, so I'd turned it into my own time capsule. An assortment of masterful stick-figure drawings and fortune cookie papers lay beneath beaded jewelry I'd made before I was allowed to create the real thing. Various beach treasures gave it all a briny seaside perfume.

Afraid I'd be discovered any minute, I hurried to wrap each piece of jewelry in its own velvet cloth and lay them inside. As I carried the emerald necklace to the hole in the floor, I hesitated. The essence of the spirits still attached to the jewels yearned for a sense of peace, to be righted.

I shook off the sensation. This wasn't the time to let my emotions get the best of me. *Keep a level head,* I reminded myself and added the necklace to the sordid collection.

Once I'd replaced the floorboard, I decided to start my investigation with my original plan: find the missing jewelry, find the killer—hopefully. Not that there couldn't be a variety of other reasons to kill someone, but a small fortune in jewelry was a pretty good one. It seemed smartest to start there.

I grabbed our record binder and reviewed the list of missing jewelry I'd compiled the day before. My best bet was searching for them close to home, seeing as how Wyatt clearly hadn't made it off the island. Our rival town, Serenity, had a few pawn shops and consignment stores, but it was an hour's drive north along the rugged coast. Since I was short on both time and wheels, I called around.

While a couple of businesses said they'd recently purchased secondhand jewelry, a few simple questions eliminated them from my list. Of course, Serenity wasn't completely in the clear. There was a chance the shop owners were lying, but visiting them in person was a low priority.

At lunchtime, I ran back to the house to whip up a meal for

my dad and me: canned soup and sandwiches, the extent of my cooking skills after five years without a proper kitchen. When we'd finished, I returned to hit the local shops.

As I cruised the familiar streets, my footsteps thudded with warm wooden sounds. When the town was first developed, each new store vied for the best seaside view, building closer and closer to the cliffs until they eventually stuck out beyond them on piers and docks. It resulted in the entire downtown core being interconnected by a maze of boardwalks. While the odd vehicle had access for deliveries or emergencies, the thoroughfares were meant for pedestrians.

Standing at the top of Orca Avenue, I dreaded the task ahead of me. The uneven curve to the harbor's horseshoe meant it was choked with winding streets, dead ends, and secret back-alley shops. It seemed mysterious and magical when you wanted to window shop, but it also meant I had my work cut out for me.

I just had to stick to my task, ask my questions, and get out of each store. No getting sucked into idle chitchat or local gossip. It wasn't like I was going to be around for long, anyway. I'd solve the case, my dad would heal, and I'd get out of everyone's hair again.

My throat tightened. I tried to clear it, but the sensation spread across my chest, making it hard to breathe. Was leaving still the best thing for everyone? It hadn't turned out so great for my dad the first time around.

One thing at a time, I told myself. *Keep it together.*

My first stop was Mew to You, a cat-themed consignment shop. The free-spirited woman who owned the place sold a variety of new and used clothing, accessories, and knickknacks, usually covered in the hair of the store's mascots: her three cats.

When I entered, a tabby announced my arrival with a frightening yowl. Who needed door chimes when you had a guard cat?

Pepper Moon popped up from behind the counter and adjusted her purple-framed glasses. "Is that Violet Woods?"

I approached the counter. "Hi, Pepper."

"Well, I'll be." She shook her head, dreamcatcher earrings jangling. "I haven't seen you around here in…"

"Five years." But, of course, she knew that. The shop-keepers had their own gossip ring. "I'm back to help my dad with the store."

"Of course. I hope he's doing okay." She clicked her tongue. "The attack is a sign of how Hope's been changing lately. More and more seasonal workers coming and going. And did you hear about the resort they're building? Soon, you won't even recognize your neighbors." She pulled her crocheted shawl closer around her. "The break-in has us all on edge. If thieves targeted one shop, who's to say any of us are safe?"

While that was true, a jewelry store would be the most obvious target. I wasn't sure why a thief would break in to, say, the craft or knitting store, but I wasn't up to date on the demand for locally spun yarn on the black market.

With so many places on my list to visit, I didn't want to beat around the bush. "I popped by to see if any jewelry has come in lately."

Pepper gave me a knowing look that got my hopes up until she said, "That's smart, but none of your jewels have come through here. You're welcome to have a poke around, though. Fifty percent off winter stock." She swept an arm at the sale rack, nearly knocking some clutter off the counter with her shawl.

"Maybe something came in when you weren't working."

"I'm sorry, darling. My part-timer would have said some-thing because I approve all inventory purchases. I'll let you know if anyone comes in to sell jewelry."

My posture slumped. Not that I thought investigating would be that easy, but one could always hope. "Great, thanks.

I'm going to check a few other places around town, just in case."

She tilted her head. "It can't hurt. But us shopkeepers look out for one another. I'm certain if any jewelry was being pawned off, someone would have notified the sheriff by now."

"Well, I'm not about to ask him," I muttered. "We're not exactly best friends at the moment."

She wrinkled her nose. "I heard he's giving your dad a hard time. And it wouldn't surprise me if Mayor Abernathy's nipping at his heels too. Tell me, has he popped by Charming Treasures to take measurements for renovations yet?"

I'd been slowly backing away, ready to continue my search. At her words, I rooted to the spot. "The mayor? What do you mean?"

"He's been breathing down your poor dad's neck for years, trying to buy the place. Getting pushy about it too. Who can blame him with your location and square footage?" She looked around her own place like she wouldn't mind a change of scenery. "With your dad in trouble, Abernathy's probably rubbing his palms together, waiting for things to fall apart so he can swoop in."

"I wasn't aware of that." However, it shed new light on why he'd asked about my dad's shop when I'd seen him on the ferry.

Pepper lowered her voice even though we were alone. Well, except for her cats. "It's not only your place he's got his eye on. He's on a mission to acquire half the downtown real estate for his big campaign. Calls it 'Hope for the Future.'" She made a disgusted throaty sound. "Clever name, but it sounds like a load of fish guts."

If taking over our shop was part of a grand plan, just how far would he go to make it happen? He could have paid Wyatt to rob the store then killed him to cover his tracks. Or maybe I just wanted my almost-father-in-law to be involved.

Even if Mayor Abernathy was capable of murder, he

wouldn't have done the dirty work himself. And questioning him personally would be pointless—and, frankly, terrifying. I had to search for the person who'd done the actual deed.

I leaned on the counter. "What does the mayor plan on doing with all the property he buys?"

"He says he wants to ramp up tourism. I suspect that means commercialize Hope. Next thing you know, we'll have chain stores coming in here." Pepper banged on the counter. "I'm telling you, Violet. Don't sell. Don't let him win, or we all lose."

"I promise. I won't let that happen." Because it would mean I'd failed my mission, and that wasn't an option.

Thanking her, I left Mew to You to continue my search for the stolen jewels. But hours later, I stumbled out of the last shop on my list empty-handed. It was almost five p.m. Closing time. While I wasn't ready to quit for the day, what else could I do? I didn't have my finger on Hope's pulse anymore.

Lucy Litton would be a wealth of information, but we weren't exactly BFFs in high school, and I hadn't gotten the memo anything had changed. Besides, going to her for information would only draw unwanted attention to my investigation and give her more fodder for her next article.

As I rested in the promenade's gazebo, which was often used as a bandstand in the summer, a thought hit me. Or, rather, a scent. It smelled like sweet, warm comfort: baked goods.

Only one baker could make something smell that good. My actual BFF, Alice. And what better place to learn about recent gossip than the local bakery called Spread the Word?

CHAPTER TEN

As the four-sided post clock on the promenade struck five p.m., I rushed down Beluga Boulevard to a yellow clapboard storefront. Spread the Word was squished between the bookstore and the kids' toy store—talk about prime real estate for sweet treats. Breathless, I arrived as Alice was flipping over the Sorry We're Closed sign.

The peppy brunette spotted me through the glass door and swung it open. "Hey, stranger!"

I beamed at her. "Long time no see."

She opened her arms for a hug, and I fell into them, lingering for an extra-long squeeze. While we'd talked and emailed frequently over the years, it wasn't the same as hanging out in person.

Grinning from ear to ear, Alice pulled away. "I'm so happy you're back. I would have come by to see you, but I thought you'd want some alone time with your dad first. Want to come in and catch up?"

"Is it okay that I'm here after close?" I asked. "You won't get in trouble with your boss?"

She rolled her eyes and yanked me inside. "What Roman

doesn't know won't hurt him. Besides, he owes me. We're short-staffed, so I had to work the front all day, and now, I have to stay late for tomorrow's prep. I could use the company."

Alice slipped behind the counter, where a few leftover goodies glowed inside the lit glass case. "Would you like a French lavender-and-lemon cupcake?" She indicated the purple dessert that resembled an intricate piece of art. "Lavender is very relaxing, and you look like you could use one."

My laugh sounded more like a sigh. "Is it that obvious?"

"It's written all over your face," she said. "And whenever you're stressed, you twist your hair around your finger like that."

I dropped the copper strand. The spiral remained tight like I'd taken a curling iron to it. I must have done it a few times already. "If I need anything, it's something to perk me up. I've got a lot on my plate, and none of it is as delicious as those treats look."

Pursing her lips, she perused the case. "Then how about peppermint mocha madness?"

My mouth began to water. "Sounds perfect."

Alice plopped the chocolate delight onto a plate, and I followed her through the swinging doors into the kitchen. Compared to the front, which was painted a cheery yellow with glass cases gleaming beneath bright chandeliers, the back was drab and utilitarian. Aged floral tile with dingy grout covered the walls, and a fluorescent light swung precariously overhead.

My friend plopped a stool in front of the stainless steel counter that stretched down the middle of the area. I took a seat and wasted no time digging into my cupcake, relishing the rich mocha-and-peppermint combo. Maybe I'd just been due for a pick-me-up, but I swore I felt a renewed sense of focus for solving the murder. Must have been the peppermint and caffeine.

While I ate, I watched in amazement as Alice moved around the kitchen in a practiced dance. With no recipe in sight, she grabbed ingredients, throwing them together as though by instinct. And here I was, barely able to cobble together a grilled cheese.

"I didn't think it was possible," I said, "but you're even faster than you used to be."

She sprinkled sugar into her mixing bowl. "I had no choice. Ever since we lost Peg to retirement, I'm the only baker. Roman works me to the bone to keep up with demand. And it's not like he helps out around here." She fake-gasped at the scandalous idea. "He might get his hands dirty."

I giggled at her dramatics. "Why do you stick around?"

"Spread the Word is the only bakery in town, unless you count the bread shop, but that's not enough variety for me. I love baking, and I can't imagine doing anything else for a living."

"You were born for it." I licked some icing off my lips. "Have you considered starting your own business?"

"That's the dream." She turned on the mixer and watched it rotate. "But it's a big step, and I'd have to leave this job. I don't imagine Roman would continue to employ his direct competition. Besides, he's talked about me buying into this place and becoming a business partner."

I shook my half-eaten cupcake at her. "With baked goods this addictive, I'm certain his customers will follow you wherever you go."

"Thanks." She ducked her head.

Alice never saw the talent in herself that was clear to everyone else, but I dropped the subject of her own business. I'd planted the seed. Maybe I'd coax the idea to grow while I was around. However long that was for.

She scattered flour onto the counter. "I bet your dad's happy you're home. What's it like being back?"

"Strange." Focusing on my plate, I picked at the leftover crumbs. "It feels comfortable, but I'm afraid I'll grow too comfortable and get trapped here."

"Would that be so bad? Once you've been here a while, things will get better. It didn't help that a dead body crashed your welcome-home."

I cringed. "So you heard?"

"Jason told me what happened." She shrugged. "A perk of being the deputy's cousin is access to the best gossip." A huge smile spread across her heart-shaped face. "I'm so proud of him. He's really turned his life around."

"He seems to love his new job," I said, wishing I didn't have a front-row seat to watch him in action.

Jason's start in life had been rough. He'd never known his dad. The deadbeat had wanted nothing to do with him. After Jason's mom passed away when he was a kid, he'd moved to Hope to live with his aunt, Alice's mom. The two of them grew up together like siblings. He'd gone through a bit of a rough patch, but he seemed to have pulled through it just fine.

"Look on the bright side," Alice said. "After the reception you had, at least things can only get better."

"I'm not so sure about that."

I considered requesting a soothing lavender cupcake as I dove into explaining my dad's predicament. I didn't mention him dipping his toe into insurance fraud, though. Alice might have been my closest friend, but I wanted to keep his momentary lapse in judgment to myself. Plus, since she was the deputy's cousin, I didn't want to put her in the tough spot of keeping the secret.

She pressed a hand to her chest, leaving a flour handprint behind. "Your poor dad. How can the sheriff think he's capable of something like that?"

"I suppose he's just doing his job," I said, still unconvinced. "But I figure it's because he doesn't have any other leads at the moment."

Lips pulling into a firm line, she turned off the mixer and tipped the sticky ball onto the counter. "Give it time. I'm sure the sheriff will find the real murderer."

Easy for her to say. She didn't know the whole story. True to my promise to Nolan, I'd never told her everything about the night of the accident or all the reasons I felt Reed couldn't investigate his way out of a fishing net. Nor did she know about the added complication of the altered jewels, so it was hard to explain my doubts.

"Maybe he will eventually," I said. "But my dad doesn't need this stress, and until his name is cleared, it's bad for business. The sheriff is just one man, and this is a town of five thousand. I figure the more people asking questions, the better."

She raised an eyebrow at me. "People? As in you?"

"Perhaps." I batted my eyelashes innocently. "And since I've been away so long, I hoped you might have some ideas. I didn't even know this Wyatt Thorn guy."

"Neither did I." She flattened her dough ball. "Not personally, anyway. But considering the circles he ran in, I'd be careful. He spent a lot of time at Killer Ale. The bar hasn't changed since you left. It's as seedy and divey as it's always been. Not the kind of place you want to visit solo."

"Perfect." I hopped to my feet, excited to have a new direction. "Do we know anybody who frequents there? Someone who might have been friends with the guy?"

"Well, there is one person who would be helpful." She bit her lip. "Max Nicolas."

"You're kidding. Max hangs out in a place like that?" Then I recalled his argument on the ferry. Maybe it wasn't so shocking.

Alice concentrated on her dough. "A few things have changed around here since you've been gone. Nolan's death affected this whole town, Max most of all. He didn't take it well. Became a regular at the bar, even clashed with the sheriff a few times. He gave up on the photography thing too."

"He did?" My chest grew tight, and I rubbed my fist against it. "But he wanted to sell his work."

"After the accident, he gave up on a lot of things, and it wasn't only because he lost Nolan." She pointed a rolling pin in my direction so I didn't miss her meaning. "I'm usually here until ten o'clock. On my way home, I see him walk over to Killer Ale from the marina nearly every night. He lives on his boat full time now and makes a living as a carpenter. He does beautiful work."

I thought about popping by to visit him, but it only conjured memories of the last time I'd been on his sailboat, of his confession, those sweet and regrettable words that could never be unsaid.

To hide any emotions flitting across my face, I crumpled the cupcake wrapper and tossed it into the garbage. "Is there anyone else I can talk to?"

"Not that wouldn't draw attention to you Sherlock Holmesing all over town. From what I've heard, Wyatt wasn't exactly an angel. If you go digging in the wrong places, I'm afraid you'll get hurt."

I wrapped a finger around a strand of my hair. "I'm sure I'll come up with another idea."

Alice frowned but busied herself by rolling out her dough paper smooth. "You know, Max has a sweet tooth, so he comes in here sometimes. He asks about you. When I tell him how you're doing, he seems relieved."

My finger froze in the middle of tugging on my hair. "He does?"

She gave me a sad smile. "We all feel that way. As much as I've missed you, I'm happy you're out there living life, moving on."

"Right," I said. However, the longer I was home, the more I realized that couldn't be further from the truth.

"You should talk to Max. And I don't mean about Wyatt. I know he'd be happy to see you."

I thanked Alice and told her I needed to get back to Dad. As I was leaving, she twisted my rubber arms and forced a box of cupcakes into them. Instead of going home, I found myself walking in the opposite direction. As though my legs were on autopilot, I ended up back at the promenade, looking down on the marina.

Leaning against the wooden railing, I eyed the boats bobbing along the docks. It took a minute to spot the one I was searching for because it had received a facelift since I'd seen it last. The peeling red paint had been replaced with a rich navy blue, the tattered sails with crisp white ones, but I'd have recognized the *Crescent* anywhere. When Max inherited the vessel from his father, his goal had been to fix it up. At least he hadn't let go of that dream.

Again, I considered Alice's advice about going to talk to him and brushed it aside. Even if it meant uncovering clues about Wyatt's killer, I couldn't bring myself to face him. Or maybe I couldn't face the memories of his confession, the emotions his words had stirred inside me.

A lot had changed since I'd left, but what if my feelings hadn't? What if his had?

I pushed it aside. If I was going to solve the case, I needed to remain levelheaded and avoid all those messy feelings. Besides, nothing could ever happen between me and Nolan's best friend.

Switching my focus, I considered the long structure next to the marina, jutting from the mainland on its own pier. Killer Ale. If Wyatt had hung out at the bar, then my answers might be there too. I checked the time on the post clock, now glowing as the daylight faded. It was six. They probably weren't even open yet, and if I arrived too early, asking sober people questions, I'd stick out like a sore thumb.

While I knew I should go home and eat the last of the

lasagna with Dad, restless energy bounced around inside me. Some of that might have been my frosting-covered dinner, but it was mostly my intuition urging me toward Charming Treasures, where the emeralds hid. They were calling me, and it was time I answered them.

CHAPTER ELEVEN

The moment I walked into the family shop, I sensed the wrongness of the redesigned jewelry tug at me. My other-worldly connection had never felt so strong before. I locked the door then followed the silent call into the back, to the secret compartment. When I lifted the floorboard and plucked out the ugly pendant, the emeralds practically screamed for me to fix them. And that was exactly what I planned to do.

If the sheriff were ever to discover them, he'd probably assume he'd caught the bad guy, case closed. While Dad's only crime was considering insurance fraud, it would still incriminate him in Wyatt's death. I needed to return them to their original setting, or close enough to it. Then, at least we could fall back on the "Gee whiz, they weren't lost after all" defense.

Would fixing them really be so wrong?

I mentally slapped myself. Of course it would be. Tampering with evidence was illegal. Yet it didn't feel wrong to protect my father. That felt like the most honorable thing in the world to do.

As I carried the emerald necklace to my old workstation, my skin crawled as though I were being watched. I whirled around. A figure stood in the doorway to the front of the store.

Gasping, I clutched the necklace to my chest. But it was only Nolan. I heaved a sigh until I saw he wasn't alone. The little black cat coiled around his ghostly legs. I ran to check the front door, but it was still locked.

Strange. Had the cat slipped past me on the way in?

Well, it looked like I had an audience. It could have been worse. At least Wyatt wasn't there to witness what I was about to do. Still, I bit the inside of my cheek as I met Nolan's gaze, expecting to see judgment, maybe because I felt I deserved it. Instead, he cocked his head with a wry look on his perfect features. I took it as a sign of support.

For the first time, I didn't wish he'd go away. I wheeled my father's leather chair over to my workstation and positioned it next to mine. Nolan understood the invitation and sat. Finally, I was on the same page with a ghost. Or, even in death, my fiancé just *got* me.

Nolan's cat, as I'd come to think of her, leaped onto the workbench and curled up to watch me. Bolstered by the presence of my partners in crime, I reached for my tools on autopilot.

Dad hadn't touched a thing since I'd left. I found a few pieces of ready-made settings, filigree embellishments, my saw blades, and everything else still organized in the wooden drawers that sat on top of my jeweler's bench.

It felt so right to be creating again, as natural as breathing. For as long as I could remember, it was what I'd wanted to do. As a child, I'd doodle in class, dreaming up designs to make once Dad taught me the trade. That sense of wonder had never left, and as I worked now, I felt the tension in my body melt away.

Once I'd liberated the emeralds from their deformed bonds, I reached out to them. Not physically but as though my spirit shook the hand of the soul's essence that still clung to it. It felt familiar.

I recalled when I'd purchased the original earring and

pendant set from a hole-in-the wall jewelry shop in Paris. More like I remembered the elderly woman who'd been haunting the place. As with other ghosts, I'd ignored her, and I asked the store clerk to show me a lovely silver-and-emerald necklace. The moment I touched it, the shop swelled with an alarming holler that stole the breath from my lungs.

Nearly dropping the pendant, I spun around. The noise was coming from the ghost. With an arthritic finger pointed in my direction, she yelled something at me. I actually heard her. Sadly, I couldn't understand her, since my French was abysmal.

The clerk gave me a strange look. "Are you all right, miss?"

Swallowing, I tried to shake it off, which was hard to do with someone screaming in my ear. "Yes. I'm sorry. May I see the matching earrings?"

With a flourish, he produced them, and the ghost wailed on. I examined the pieces with a jeweler's eye, but as I held them, something else bubbled to the surface. The ghost's presence still lingered on them like a whisper of perfume. Beneath that, I sensed the many generations of women who'd worn the jewels before her.

I suddenly appreciated the spirit's outrage. They were very old and precious, and she didn't want to part with them, even in death. The shop owner clearly wasn't aware of the set's value, and I felt guilty when I bought them at a steal. After I left, the elderly ghost followed me down the street, cursing at me—I'd learned a few of those words. I wished I could help her find peace, but she didn't seem in a peaceful mood.

Now, seated at my jeweler's bench, I communicated with the emeralds. The personality radiating from them was bold and feisty, the way the ghost had felt. These three stones did not belong mashed together into one pendant. They wanted to be celebrated independently, as they had been before.

"Don't worry," I told them. "You'll be back to yourselves soon enough."

I hadn't realized how much I'd missed making jewelry. It

was as though inspiration had coiled inside me, waiting to spring the moment I touched my tools again. Resisting my creative whims, I used the photo in our record binder and stuck as close to the original designs as my limited time and supplies allowed me.

Finally, the set was complete, and the unsettled spirits attached to them calmed. I compared them to the set in the picture. Of course, the sheriff would never notice the difference, but if he consulted a skilled jeweler, then we might be in trouble. But he'd have to find the gems first.

"What do you think?" I asked Nolan.

He raised his eyebrows and nodded in exaggerated seriousness. I was so well acquainted with his silly humor that I could imagine him saying, "In my impeccable, nonexpert opinion, I'd say it's… jewelry."

I laughed. Then I remembered myself and the situation. A wave of grief weighed down my sudden joy. I smothered it and turned to pet the cat, focusing on the softness of her fur, something real and tangible.

When I pulled away, she meowed, like *Did I give you permission to stop?*

"What are we going to call you? I can't keep thinking of you as 'cat.'" She really looked so much like Nolan's old pet. "Maybe Zelda Junior?"

She purred.

"Zelda it is. We should get you home so you can sleep somewhere warm tonight until I find your owner. Either way, you can't come to Killer Ale with me. Something tells me even a dive bar doesn't allow animals. Not the furry kind, anyway."

After adding the restored emeralds to the hidden compartment, I replaced the floorboards and set a chair on top of them —like that was going to make all the difference in the world. By the time I'd cleaned up my station and walked out of the shop with the box of cupcakes, I felt lighter than I had in a long time.

On my way out, I held the door open for Zelda to slip out and automatically waited for Nolan to exit despite his ability to walk through solid objects. In the glow of the promenade lights, I fished out my key. While I was locking up, shoes scuffed against wood behind me.

Zelda arched her back and hissed.

I whipped around. Someone was standing on the boardwalk behind me. I backpedaled until I hit the door, rattling the windows in their lead frames.

Gold flashed on the man's chest. A badge.

Sheriff Reed tipped his hat. A quirk to his lips hinted at a triumphant smile, like *Aha! I caught you.* Or else that was my guilt-ridden imagination.

"Good evening, Miss Woods. You're here awfully late."

My back went rigid, and I was certain the box of cupcakes was trembling in my hands. Could he tell? "I'm sorry. We're closed. You'll have to purchase your new belly ring another day."

He drew closer until the light was at his back, his expression cast in shadow—not that he'd have been an open book otherwise. "I was in the area and noticed the lights on, so I came by to ask for the updated inventory list."

"I don't have it yet. The place was a mess, and the files are all handwritten. It's going to take time to sort through it all."

He placed his fists on his hips, drawing my attention to his gun. "I shouldn't have to explain to you how important it is. A man died."

"So I noticed. But what does that have to do with our inventory?" Unless he was hoping to find exactly what I'd feared, what I'd hidden beneath the floorboards. He must have been tracking the missing jewelry to sniff out the killer, just like me. However, if he searched the shop, he'd pick up the completely wrong scent.

Reed stepped onto the bottom stair. "In the meantime, I

was hoping to have another look around and take a few more photos."

Nolan shifted to stand between us, as though he might protect me. The light from the nearby lamppost turned his body diaphanous, and it distorted the sheriff like a funhouse mirror.

"Why would you need to do that?" I asked innocently. "Didn't you get all the photos you needed after the break-in?"

The sheriff rose another step. "Never hurts to get a few fresh ones."

I maintained my frozen position in front of the door. "Except that I've cleaned the worst of the mess, so it won't help you. Unless this isn't about the robbery anymore." I dropped down a step until I was eye level with him. "It sounds like this is about a murder investigation in which my father is a suspect. And if you don't have a warrant to show me, you're not getting inside this building."

He sucked on his teeth, mustache wiggling, as he studied me.

That's right, Sheriff Reed. Check and mate.

Finally, he said, "You're going to make this difficult, aren't you?"

"Did you expect me to make it easy for you? You didn't make life easy for me after I lost my fiancé." I smiled sweetly. "I'm only returning the favor. Come back when you have a warrant."

He narrowed his cool blue eyes. "You can count on it. See you real soon." He tipped his hat then strode across the promenade, footfalls echoing around the deserted space.

As I watched him leave, I wondered how long he'd been lurking out there. It was a good thing I hadn't tried to move the jewels elsewhere; I wasn't a good enough actress to have gotten past him. And now, I definitely couldn't move them. Who knew if he'd come back or if Jason was out there, spying on the place?

Zelda slunk down the steps, her twitching tail mirroring the anxiety I felt. Her eyes glowed eerily beneath the antique lamppost as she shifted her furry head toward Nolan. Their gazes locked, and his mouth moved soundlessly before he gave her a nod. Then she turned and padded after the sheriff.

My mouth fell open. Did they just… interact? I shook it off. No. That was ridiculous.

Wrapping my jacket tighter around me, I got moving. It wouldn't be long before the sheriff returned with a warrant, and I suspected he'd be thorough searching the place. Although I wasn't ready to face Max, I no longer had the luxury of time, and he was my best and quickest option to get answers. I guessed I was going for a drink.

CHAPTER TWELVE

I arrived at Killer Ale just before eleven p.m. I hoped I wasn't too late, that Max hadn't already been there and left. However, the low thud of music and rowdy shouts drifting out told me the place was just picking up. Avoiding a dark patch dripping down the wall and onto the pier, I tried to peek through the porthole-like windows, but they were blacked out. There was no preparing for whatever waited inside.

I wished I'd begged Alice to join me. Even though Nolan would have been some form of company, I'd snuck away when he wasn't looking. It was for the best. Whatever Max had to say to me after so many years, I didn't want my fiancé to hear it.

A cool breeze blew off the water. For a dive bar, it had a prime location, jutting out on the pier for an unobstructed view. No one in town minded, though, since it was situated higher than the promenade and blocked the small fishing harbor and cannery on the other side. And as long as you didn't look too closely, the building was clean enough and kept in line with the town's cheerful seaside-town theme.

At the entrance, I was greeted with a toothy grin and a wink by the bar's most famous regular: Ollie the Orca. The black-and-white killer whale had been carved by a local woodworking artist and was at least three times my size. It leaped overhead while drinking a bottle of, you guessed it, ale.

As I pushed open the double wooden doors, a waft of stale alcohol hit me. While the tables in the middle sat empty, patrons filled the dark booths that hugged the walls, having intimate yet loud conversations. What was it about alcohol that affected volume control?

"Evening," a deep voice rumbled.

I jumped away from a muscular man perched on a stool next to the door. He wore a long-sleeved shirt that was so tight it could have passed for cling wrap.

A bouncer on a Thursday night? Maybe Alice had been right and I shouldn't have come alone.

He gave me the once over, not in a mildly flattering way but with suspicion. Finally, he tilted his head to the side and turned away. Permission to enter, I supposed. I was glad I'd worn my black leather jacket I'd purchased at a night market in Florence. At least I passed for someone who might belong here.

Eyes followed me as I walked up to the bar, my calf-high boots sticking to the beer-lacquered floor. The people who I didn't recognize looked wary of a newcomer. Those I did probably wondered what Violet Woods was doing in a place like Killer Ale.

While I wasn't the same person who'd been about to marry the town's golden boy, it was hard to change people's view of you in a small town. Poor Jason Swan would be a teenage troublemaker until the day he died.

Ignoring the stares, I grabbed a stool at the far end of the bar to survey the room. Chandeliers made from old ship wheels hung from the building's exposed rafters, but their dim light barely reached the corners of the large space. As my eyes adjusted, I scanned the ruddy faces lit by nautical lanterns above each booth. Max wasn't among them. I hoped Alice was right about him coming most nights.

"What can I get you?" a smooth voice asked.

I turned on my stool to face the bartender. A woman a few years younger than me leaned against the other side of the bar. She gave me a friendly smile with red lips that matched the colorful streak in her black, waist-length braids.

I'd never met her in my life, and yet something about her looked familiar. No. Not looked. *Seemed*. There was no other way to explain it.

While I needed to keep my wits about me, I figured a drink would help me blend in better. "Vodka soda with the lime, please."

"Coming right up." She set a glass in front of her and grabbed the bottles without looking. "I haven't seen you around here before. You new in town?"

"Old to town, actually. I've been away for a few years. Just got in yesterday."

After measuring out the vodka, she dumped in extra anyway. "Welcome home. What brings you back?"

"Family stuff." I couldn't exactly get into it, so I rolled my eyes as if to say *You know how it is,* hoping she'd leave it at that.

She slid the full glass in front of me. "And you're already here for a drink? Sounds like we might be from the same family."

She wasn't wrong about the drink part. Right now, it was exactly what I needed.

I observed the young woman as she replaced the bottles. I knew I should circulate, check if Max was lurking in one of the corner booths or in the back room, where pool balls clacked. However, I couldn't shake the odd vibe I was getting from her.

I sipped my drink. "How long have you lived in Hope?"

"Not long. I moved here a couple years ago from San Diego. Came to work the tourist season and never left." She stuck out a hand. "I'm Roxy, by the way."

"Violet," I said, shaking it. "So, what made you want to stay?"

"Honestly? A man." Her mouth twisted as though she'd licked a used coffee filter. She filled a glass with water and took a swig to wash away some bitter memory. "Why did you want to leave?"

I quirked an eyebrow. "I suppose… a man."

"Then, here's to love." She raised her glass.

Laughing, I returned the gesture and drank deeply.

She grabbed a cloth and wiped the drops of vodka she'd left on the counter. As she leaned forward, a pendant fell out from beneath her low neckline. I tried to study it without coming off as creepy. Then I nearly spat my drink out all over the bar.

It was a ruby pendant. One of the pieces stolen from the store. I'd have known it anywhere, because I'd picked it out myself in Greece.

That's why the bartender seemed familiar. I hadn't been sensing her but my connection to the jewel itself.

Thumping my chest, I choked down my mouthful before coughing into my sleeve.

Roxy wrinkled her nose. "Sorry. I tend to be generous with the liquor. My boss gives me a hard time about it, but the tips are always better."

I cleared my throat. "No. This is great. It just went down the wrong tube." I took another swallow to soothe both my throat and my nerves. It was detective time. "That's a pretty necklace, and I know a nice piece of jewelry when I see one. I'm a bit of a collector." Which wasn't technically a lie.

"Oh, thank you. I just got it." She lowered her gaze to the bar top. "It was a gift."

This was it. Maybe whoever gave her the necklace had killed Wyatt. Or at least he might have been an accomplice, either in the robbery or in his murder. This investigating thing wasn't so hard after all.

I made what I hoped was a scandalized gossipy sound. "Ooh. A boyfriend?"

Roxy shrugged it off like it was no big deal, but her blush said otherwise. "It was only a thoughtful gift from a friend. He's really sweet. Sweeter than my last boyfriend, not that he set a high bar to beat."

I leaned on the sticky counter. "You're talking about the one you stayed in Hope for?"

"Yeah. He was a real jerk. I left my life in San Diego for him, and he strung me along for over a year. I thought he loved me, even when he was stealing money out of my purse to cover his debts. I feel naive now, but I've got a soft spot for bad boys."

I nodded sagely. "I hear you." However, the truth was, I'd started dating Nolan in high school, so I didn't have any bad-boy experience. He'd been a prince.

"My ex was full of promises." Roxy lowered her voice an octave, her expression serious. "'One day, we're gonna travel, baby. I'm going to show you the world. Just wait. Big things are coming for us.'" She dropped the fake tone. "Then, one night, I came home to find him passed out, clutching his old wedding album. He wasn't over his ex. I was a distraction, a rebound."

"That sucks. You deserve better than that." And I meant it, but I wanted to learn more about the new guy, not the old one.

"You bet I do." She threw the cloth onto the counter. "So I taught him a lesson. No one treats Roxy that way." Her lips curved into an impish grin, and her eyebrow piercing wiggled up and down like a secret told in Morse code.

While it had obviously been a rough breakup, by the satisfied look on her face, I wasn't sure who'd had it worse in the end.

"That has to be tough in a small town where you're always bumping into exes. Hopefully, this new guy will turn out better." I leaned in. "What's his name?"

As she opened her mouth to answer, someone stepped up to the bar. Already grabbing a glass, she turned to take his order.

So close.

Annoyed, I checked out the newcomer. It took me a moment to place him, but once he leaned against the bar, it took me back to the ferry. He was the captain.

Roxy gave him a chin tilt in greeting. "Hey, Elijah. You're in later than usual tonight. What can I get you?"

He tossed his knitted hat down on the bar. "Where have you been? I've been calling you since yesterday."

Her head jerked back at his tone. "I've been out of cell range for a couple days. You know how crummy the service is around here. Got back into town today, and I was running late for work, so I haven't checked my voicemails."

His attention slid my way, and I pretended to check my phone, trying to give off a *don't worry about me* air. I almost began whistling.

Leaning closer to Roxy, he lowered his voice. "Where were you?"

"Busy. What's it to you?"

"You haven't heard?" He patted his wind-tossed russet hair. "I guess it's better coming from me. You should sit down."

She threw him an exasperated look. "I'm already skating on thin ice after coming in late. The boss would have my head if I took a break now. But please, keep me in suspense. I've got all night."

Taking his own advice, Elijah sat one stool over from me and pointed to the beer on tap. He clearly wasn't worried about her break anymore. As she poured him a drink, he muttered to himself.

"I should have expected something like this. I could have done more. Then maybe he wouldn't be…"

Roxy slammed the beer down in front of him and took in his expression. "You're freaking me out. Just spit it out already."

"Wyatt's dead, Rox."

Her tough-girl mask cracked. "How? When?"

"Not sure exactly. He was found washed up yesterday

morning when I came back from my first run." He glanced at me again, and this time, his expression lit up with recognition. "He was discovered by her, actually."

I stiffened, feeling guilty for some reason, like I'd done the deed myself. When Roxy's wide eyes locked on mine, the intense urge to apologize rushed through me.

"I'm so sorry. I had no idea you knew him. Was he your friend? The one who gave you that necklace?" He might have given it to her before the murder.

Her face twisted with a sneer. "No way. Wyatt was the jerk who broke my heart." The anger dropped away as quickly as it had come on, and she blinked away tears. "No. That's not right to say. He's dead. It's just… you say and do things you regret, and you think you'll have a chance to make things right."

What kinds of things did she regret doing? Strangling him with a rope and dumping his body in the ocean, perhaps? The woman obviously had unresolved feelings about their breakup. And where had she been that kept her out of cell range for so long?

Sure, she was acting genuinely shocked, but that could have been because I'd found the body when she'd hoped it would have been shark food by now. She did say she'd taught him a lesson.

While it was a huge step forward in my case—I had an actual suspect—the fact that the necklace had come from someone else was even bigger. Girl talk was over, but I had to try one last time.

"So, if not Wyatt, who gave you that necklace?"

Her unfocused gaze homed in on me, and she tilted her head as though seeing me for the first time. I swallowed, trying not to shrink back. Thankfully, the entrance door squeaked open behind me, and her interest shifted toward it.

The tension in her body leaked out, and the sadness in her expression melted away. "Speak of the devil."

Nearly giving myself whiplash, I turned. Walking into Killer Ale like he owned the place was Max Nicolas.

I wanted to dive over the bar to hide behind it. However, Max didn't look our way. Instead, he spotted someone in a corner booth, the floppy-haired deckhand he'd been fighting with on the ferry. I searched my memory for his name: Christian.

They gave each other a solemn nod, and Max joined him. The two men didn't strike me as friends meeting for a drink. They clearly hadn't worked things out yet.

My brain whirled with new questions. How did Max get his hands on the stolen jewelry? Was he in on the robbery, or did he have something to do with Wyatt's death? And then, to my great annoyance, I wondered if he'd given the necklace to Roxy in friendship or romance.

Elijah watched the bartender closely. "You okay, Rox? Why don't you get some air or something?"

"Yeah." She sniffed and straightened her posture. "You're right."

I dug a bill out of my purse and laid it on the counter. "Thanks for the drink. Keep the change."

Roxy gaped at the money. "Are you sure? We don't charge San Diego prices here."

"I'm sure." I felt bad for hassling her during a tough time. You know, unless she was actually Wyatt's killer.

With a swig, I downed the last of my drink and slipped out of the bar before Max spotted me. It wasn't like I could approach him and say, "Hey, long time no see. What have you been up to? Any robbing and killing?"

Alice had said he lived on his boat, so if he had any more of the jewelry, it would most likely be there. And if it was, I intended to find it. Passing beneath Ollie the Orca, I wiggled my fingers at him in farewell and marched for the marina.

CHAPTER THIRTEEN

As I navigated the maze of docks and walkways toward Max's boat, the fear I'd be caught at any moment threatened to strangle me. I passed rows of moored vessels, their hulls bumping against fenders with each gentle wave. The impacts sent vibrations shuddering beneath my feet, and I imagined someone following close behind.

Paranoid, I scanned the marina, which was lit only by the promenade's lampposts and their reflections off the water. No sign of anyone, and the surrounding boats were dark. It wasn't common for owners to live on their crafts like Max.

I didn't want to believe he might have something to do with a robbery, much less a murder. There were multiple ways he could have acquired the ruby necklace he'd given Roxy. However, I had to follow the evidence, remain levelheaded for Dad's sake. I would do anything to protect him. And, in a way, this was for Max's benefit too. If he was innocent, then I was technically proving it by searching his boat. Right? Okay, I was reaching for that excuse.

Shoving my hands into my pockets, I acted as though I were out for a stroll. *Nothing to see here, folks.* When I approached the restored navy blue sailboat, I didn't hesitate; only people who didn't belong hesitated.

I jumped aboard and strode across the teak deck to the cabin door. Holding my breath, I tried the handle and pulled. As I'd hoped, it opened.

Max wasn't a lock-the-door kind of guy. He'd always said it was because he had nothing to steal, and if someone wanted to break in to discover that, he'd rather not have to repair a busted door. Then I remembered his confrontation on the ferry. Maybe nowadays, he didn't bother locking up because people knew better than to mess with him. People with some sense, that is.

I opened the door all the way and peered inside. Now, I did hesitate. Was I really about to do this?

Sure, Max and I hadn't talked in years, and when I'd left, things were, shall we say, strained. But he'd always been a good friend, honest, and there for me.

This is for Dad, I reminded myself.

The cabin was dim. Only the moonlight flooded through the tiny water-spotted windows, filling the space with cool light. I took out my phone and turned on the flashlight function. There was no jewelry lying out in the open next to a bloody rope or anything as convenient as that, so I descended the steep stairs, plunging into the belly of the boat.

Since the last time I'd been in there, Max had ripped out the guts and replaced everything. I couldn't help but admire the love he'd put into it.

A bed sat nestled at the far end of the cabin beneath a round port window where the morning sun would shine in. The clever nooks and shelves around it were bursting with dog-eared novels. I shifted them around to search. The only thing I found was more titles to add to my to-read list.

Behind a wooden table that folded away like origami, a leather bench seat stretched along one side of the cabin. As with everything else, it was attached to the floor. Otherwise, each trip to the open sea would have resulted in an accidental redecoration.

I lifted the seat to reveal a storage compartment that contained mostly food. For good measure, I shook the cereal boxes, listening for a metallic tinkle.

A quick rummage through the modern kitchenette cupboards turned up nothing except a fastidious sense of organization. And the little bathroom was cleaner than most hostel facilities I'd had the pleasure of experiencing.

Finally, I moved to the desk built into the wall and slid open the drawer. I was surprised to find myself staring at… myself.

Among scattered bills and receipts, old pictures of Max, Nolan, and me lined the bottom, creating a collage of our friendship. Gently, I picked one up, as though it might fall apart like so much from that time already had.

The photo showed the three of us splayed out on the rocky beach at Tiptoe Point, a secluded spot where Sleeping Beauty's foot rested. We'd taken out Max's boat for the first time since he'd inherited it after his father's death.

In those last few months together, we'd explored every inch of the island's coast. Life had been so perfect back then. Until the night Nolan told me his secret and I'd come running straight into Max's arms.

Rattled after the magic I'd seen, I told Max I couldn't go through with the wedding. As Nolan's best friend, I wondered if he knew about the warlock thing, but in the end, I didn't ask. Nor did I tell him about what I'd witnessed, because my doubts were about more than that. Was I supposed to marry someone who'd lied to me for so long, someone I wasn't sure I could trust? And it wasn't only him. It was his family, their whole world I didn't belong in.

Max listened quietly, holding me when my explanation turned to sobs. When I was done, he encouraged me to talk things out with Nolan before the next morning. Just speaking with someone I trusted had calmed me, and I'd regained some equilibrium. I knew he was right.

Wiping away my tears, I turned to go find my fiancé. Before I could leave, Max drew me back, taking my hands in his large ones. My heart skipped as he considered me with his stormy blue eyes.

"But if you can't go through with it and you need to get out of here, just hop on this boat. I'll take you wherever you want to go, and we never have to come back. We can sail on forever. Whatever you decide, I will support you. Because I love you."

I pressed a palm to my chest, touched by my friend's sweet words. "I appreciate that. And I love you too."

Then he held my face, tenderly but firmly, and said it again. "I love you, Violet." And judging by the intensity in his gaze, he didn't mean as just friends.

As I stared back, speechless, the door flew open. Max and I took a guilty step apart as Nolan rushed into the cabin and breathed a sigh of relief that he'd tracked me down. He begged me to talk things out with him. Since I was even more confused than when I'd stumbled onto the boat, I let him walk me to his car.

I'd relived that moment a thousand times and still wasn't sure how I might have responded to Max's confession. And I never had a chance to, because that was the last time we'd spoken.

The longer I'd been gone, the easier it had been to ignore my life in Hope, to ignore the feelings I wasn't supposed to have for Max. I still believed my departure had been best for most people. Certainly less painful for the Abernathys and fewer reminders for others who'd loved Nolan. And that had been many.

It hadn't been best for everyone, though. Dad had struggled even more with the business. I hadn't been there to help Alice achieve her baking dreams. And now, facing the photos of all the good times Max and I'd shared, I imagined all the other memories we didn't get to make over the last five years.

After replacing the photo, I closed the drawer filled with my past and stepped away. I should have talked to him at the bar. If he'd lied about something, I would have picked up on it. He used to have this tell when he wasn't being truthful. A subtle twitch to his left eyebrow, like *I dare you to call my bluff.*

As I turned to leave, I shone my phone's light toward the exit. It glinted off polished metal. Something gold dangled from a pipe in the corner of the room.

I took a step closer. It was a pocket watch.

Dad had said a pocket watch was among the items stolen. It wasn't a common accessory these days, and Max wasn't one to accessorize.

Curious, I reached out for it. Before my fingers could brush the metal, a sound drifted into the cabin, too rhythmic to be waves lapping the hull.

Footsteps.

My body tensed, and I turned off my phone's light. *Please, don't be Max. Please, don't be Max.*

The sound drew closer, and I remembered his boat was the last one in the row. Unless someone was going for a chilly midnight swim, this was their destination.

Move, I willed my frozen limbs.

I climbed the steep stairs and squeezed out of the little door, shutting it quietly behind me. Heart pounding, I snuck around the side of the cabin and hid.

A figure stepped aboard, silhouetted by the promenade lights. Was it Max? No. The person was too short, their frame slight.

I considered holding out until they hopefully left again. However, as the fog rolling in settled on my skin and clothes, I knew I'd freeze in my leather jacket before I'd have the chance to escape. I had to make a break for it and hope I was the faster runner.

Shifting positions, I waited for my chance. The door squeaked open and closed again, then I counted down.

Three… Two… One… Now!

I sprang forward and rounded the cabin. When I was halfway across the deck, footfalls thudded close by.

My head whipped toward the sound. A dark figure rushed me. They hadn't gone inside after all.

I tried to dodge them, but they slammed into me. Stumbling back, I instinctively grabbed them. My hand clamped around something on their wrist. A bracelet.

Impressions pressed into my brain: a woman, bitter, determined. Then she shook me off and shoved me hard in the chest.

My boots skidded on the deck. They slipped out from under me, and I sailed back. I braced for impact.

When my fall continued, I realized my landing would be far worse than a hard deck. I filled my lungs with air just before I plunged into the freezing water.

Darkness swallowed me, and my muscles seized from the cold. I couldn't tell which way was up. For a panicked moment, I wondered if this was what happened to Wyatt. Had his killer just attacked me? Was I the next victim?

I kicked and thrashed until I broke the surface. Gasping for air, I wiped the salt water from my vision to get my bearings.

The hull of the boat nudged me as it rocked. I craned my neck to look up, but there was no one leering down at me from the deck. Hurried footfalls echoed across the water, and I turned to watch the mysterious figure flitting through the dim light, back to the promenade.

Well, at least I'd found the dock.

Forcing my frigid limbs to move, I fought against my heavy clothes and swam to safety. When my hand finally slapped the wooden planks, I gathered the strength to pull myself up. Before I could, a big, warm hand wrapped around my wrist.

I yelped and tried to yank away, but they hauled me out of

the water like a fish and dumped me unceremoniously onto the walkway. Shuddering, I stared wide-eyed at the man who crouched in front of me.

Between wisps of tousled black hair, a set of sharp eyes glinted in the moonlight. I recoiled until I saw they weren't filled with anger but amusement.

"Hello, Violet."

I sputtered. "M-Max."

CHAPTER FOURTEEN

Max moved around the tight cabin, his size comical compared to our tiny surroundings. He looked like a bear got stuck in a closet but much more agile. I watched him from the built-in bench seat, shivering beneath a flannel blanket. While I was still damp and cold, at least hypothermia was off the table.

He handed me a steaming mug, and I took a wary sniff. Hot chocolate.

Leaning against the counter, he regarded me as though we were near strangers. "So, to what do I owe the pleasure of your company?"

I tried to lift a shoulder, but my thawing muscles didn't respond. "Can't old friends drop in for a visit?"

"Yes. But you didn't need to be so literal about the 'drop in' part."

"Someone pushed me."

"What?" He stood a little straighter, his tough-guy act momentarily slipping. "Who would do that?"

"I didn't see. More to the point, who visiting you would do that?"

I recalled Roxy's smitten expression when she'd talked about Max. She could have used her break to come down to the marina. Maybe that was why he was back, to meet her. But then she saw another woman on the *Crescent*, jumped to conclusions, and pushed me out of jealousy. Either that or, if she knew about the stolen jewelry, she would have realized she'd let the cat out of the bag and had hoped to stop me from poking around.

Max rubbed his knuckles along his scruffy jaw, the scrape loud in the silence. "I don't know. I wasn't expecting anyone, least of all you. A bit late for a visit, don't you think?"

So we were back to that. My mouth went dry, and I took a sip of hot chocolate, scalding my tongue. "I was leaving the bar and spotted your boat. Thought I'd check if you were awake so we could catch up."

"I didn't see you there." He narrowed his eyes. "Killer Ale's not really your style."

"A lot can change in five years."

"Yes, it can," he said pointedly.

What did that mean? Did he mean me? Us? I mentally shook myself. That wasn't why I was here. *Follow the clues. Don't get emotional.*

"The bartender seemed lovely. Roxy, I think her name was." I waited but got no response. "She sure thinks highly of you. She showed me the necklace you gave her. It's a pretty piece. You must have spent a lot of money on it."

He shrugged. "It didn't cost me anything. And she's been going through a rough time lately, so I thought it might cheer her up."

It seemed like buying her a card or a coffee might have been sufficient to cheer her up and would have held fewer romantic undercurrents. While his love life was none of my business, I wondered why the necklace hadn't cost anything.

Max tilted his head. "Are you jealous?"

I nearly spilled the hot chocolate all over myself, but managed to laugh the question off. "No. It's just professional curiosity. I was wondering where you got it from."

"Why are you really here, Violet? Does it have something to do with the break-in at Charming Treasures?"

Okay, so maybe I wasn't being very subtle. Was it getting hot in there? I shook off the blanket. "That necklace was one of the stolen items."

He jerked with surprise but quickly smothered it with a cool, unreadable look. I wasn't used to this standoffish Max. I preferred the old one. Could I even trust him anymore?

Aware that we were completely alone in the marina, I stood and moved closer to the exit. "I'm just following the clues, asking questions."

He huffed. "What? Are you a PI now?"

"I'm trying to help my dad."

"So the only thing that brings you knocking on my door is a stolen necklace?" He let out an incredulous laugh that sounded more like a growl.

I stared at him, surprised by the crack in his armor. Did he want me to knock on his door for another reason? Something stirred behind my ribcage, and I mentally shushed it.

Not the time, Vi.

"The necklace isn't the only thing. There's also a missing pocket watch."

His intense focus shifted to the timepiece dangling from the pipe above my head, and when he looked back to me, the skin next to his eyes tightened. "And you think I stole it. I guess a lot does change in five years."

He took a step closer, and the cabin closed in on me. Or maybe that was because his well-built frame consumed more space than it used to. On the off chance I really was facing Wyatt's murderer, would I even have a chance against him if he tried to silence me? My phone was a waterlogged paperweight. If I screamed, would anybody hear it?

Tensing, I shrank away from him. He didn't miss it. Hurt flickered across his face.

He reached around me and unhooked the pocket watch, tossing it in my direction. "Take it. It's not my style, anyway."

As my hand closed around it, an impression hit me. Not from Max but from the watch. Regret, anger, jealousy. I shoved the piece into my pocket before I sensed more of the previous owner. I had enough of my own regrets to sort through.

"Is that all you came for?" he asked. "Or should I go get that ruby necklace back too?"

I shook my head. If it had been Roxy who'd pushed me overboard, I didn't need an even bigger target on my back. "No. I'm only trying to figure out how you got the necklace from Wyatt Thorn. He either gave it away willingly or someone took it from him. Or, rather, from his dead body."

Max took a step back, expression hardening. "I don't know why you even care about who murdered the guy. He was just some lowlife that ripped off your dad and put him in the hospital. But if you really believe someone killed him over a handful of stolen jewelry, you're only asking for trouble by sniffing around."

"Trouble has already found me. The sheriff thinks my dad might have killed Wyatt. I want to clear his name before it goes any further. So, where did you get the necklace from?"

He stared out the tiny port window, jaw working as he considered his answer. "I won it in a poker game at Killer Ale, along with the watch. By the time I got there, it had made the rounds a few times already. I don't know who brought it in the first place."

I perked up. "That's easy enough to find out. Ask the other players. Someone must have been there from the start of the game."

Max scoffed. "Killer Ale isn't a tea house. You don't go around asking questions like that."

"You do if it's the right thing to do." I gripped his arm. "Since when have you ever backed down from anyone? The Maximus Nicolas I knew fought for the little guy."

"Yeah. *Knew*. As in past tense." He pulled away, and with the cool look he gave me, it was no wonder he played poker. He probably cleaned house.

"This is my dad we're talking about." I looked him up and down. "I don't even know who you are anymore."

He turned, taking two steps before wheeling back like a caged animal with nowhere to go. "That's just it. You left. And now, five years later, you want to walk back in here and pretend you know me? Well, you don't, and you don't know this town anymore, much less the crowd at Killer Ale."

While he spoke calmly enough, the anger rolling off him swelled, filling the cabin. I swallowed hard. Okay, so he was right to be mad at me for leaving without a word. Plus, I'd been sneaking around his boat behind his back when I should have just talked to him.

"Now," he said. "You're going to drop your little investigation and let me handle things from now on. And if I see you back at the bar again, I'll have you kicked out."

Let him handle things? As if he was going to help me, this man who looked at me like we'd never been friends. Like he'd never told me he loved me.

"You're right," I said. "I don't know you anymore. And I don't think I want to."

"Fine by me." He thrust my soggy leather jacket at me.

I took it, then stomped up the steep steps and flung open the cabin door. The cool night air gave me a much-needed shake. When I went to pull on my jacket, I realized he'd also handed me a warm hooded sweatshirt. Even while he was being a stubborn jerk, he was still thoughtful. For some reason, it irritated me even more.

Yanking it over my head, I made to leave. I was halfway across the deck when I heard footsteps behind me.

"Wait!"

Despite myself, I turned back. Max closed the distance between us and thrust out a fist. I automatically flinched. Face twisting with hurt again, he kept his arm extended. He was holding something.

Hesitantly, I took it. His skin was rough and calloused, but his touch was as gentle as I remembered.

I met his gaze. My old friend was back, the boy I'd grown up with, the man who'd asked me to run off with him. A tenderness flashed across his expression before it hardened again, and he drew away.

I studied the item in my hand. It was a velvet ring box. When I raised the lid, I was stunned by the magnificent eternity band sparkling in the light from his cabin. I didn't need my microscope to know it was valuable, but it couldn't have been one of the stolen pieces from the shop; I would have recognized such a beauty from our records. So why was he giving it to me?

"What is this?" I asked.

"It's your wedding ring. Nolan gave it to me for safekeeping the day before he…" His Adam's apple bobbed. "Anyway, I wanted to give it to you, but you left the island in such a hurry, so I never had the chance. He would have wanted you to have it."

As I considered the ring again, I no longer saw its value in dollar signs. Tears blurred my vision, and my throat tightened, cutting off my response. With a *snap*, I shut the lid and shoved the box into my pocket.

I rushed off the boat and raced back to the promenade, running farther and farther away from the answers I'd been seeking. However, as hard as I'd tried, I could no longer outrun my past.

CHAPTER FIFTEEN

When I got home, it was already one a.m. I was exhausted, but I couldn't imagine going to bed. Instead, I swapped my damp clothes for dry ones, keeping on Max's sweatshirt, and slipped into the backyard. I didn't have to turn around to know Nolan was following me. He'd probably been waiting for my return.

I headed straight for the back corner of the yard where the hammock I'd spent so many summers in hung from a willow tree. Sinking into its embrace, I reflected on my conversation with Max.

My next lead was obvious: the poker game. Yet with my emotions wreaking havoc on my judgment, I felt further away from solving the puzzle. I kept recalling Max's hurt expression as I'd all but accused him of thieving or murdering.

The wedding ring weighed heavily inside my pocket. Unable to ignore its pull anymore, I removed it from the velvet box. As I placed it on my finger, I imagined Nolan doing the same on our big day. Which wasn't difficult, since he stood a few paces away in a three-piece suit.

I turned my hand this way and that so the diamonds circling the platinum band caught the moonlight. "It's beautiful," I said to myself or maybe to Nolan. "But you always did spoil me."

"You were worth spoiling," a familiar male voice came from the darkness.

I scrambled into an upright position. As I shifted my weight, the hammock swung wildly, and I overcompensated. It snapped shut like a Venus flytrap, spun upside down, and dumped me on the dewy lawn.

Ignoring the throb in my hip, I jumped to my feet. "Who's there?"

I peered into the night. Nolan and I were alone.

"Violet?" the voice came again.

My jaw slackened as the word matched the movement of Nolan's lips. I'd almost forgotten the sound of his voice, the way he spoke like he was reading poetry. Thanks to the near darkness, his ethereal form appeared solid, and as he spoke again, I could have sworn he was alive in front of me.

"Vi, can you hear me?" His green eyes danced with hope.

Slapping a hand over my mouth, I stifled a scream and backpedaled. While he seemed to grow more elated by the second, I was equally horrified. As if being haunted by his silent presence hadn't been enough.

I shook my head. "No… No. I can't."

"You can't hear me?"

My back hit the fence, and I could retreat no farther. "I mean, I can't do this. I can't talk to you right now."

The excitement on his face twisted into a grimace. "Why not? Do you know how long I've been waiting for this? For someone, anyone, to come along, and now, you won't talk to me?"

"I know it's not fair. But I'm not ready, and I don't know when I will be. I don't know anything anymore." All the built-up stress from the last few days broke through the dam I'd built, spilling from my eyes. "I don't know who took you from me or why. I don't know who killed Wyatt and how to absolve my dad. And I don't know why I ever came back here."

My legs gave out, and I sank to the grass. So much for keeping a level head.

Nolan crouched in front of me. "I can help with your dad."

I let out a shaky breath. "How can you help me? You're a ghost."

His chin lowered to his chest, and he stared at his leather shoe, which looked dry despite the dewy grass. When he didn't reply, a female voice drifted over the fence, answering instead.

"I might be older, dear, but I'm not dead yet." It was Mrs. Freeman.

I leaped to my feet and whirled to face her yard. How much had she heard? Maybe I could say I was on the phone or talking to myself.

Dashing tears away with my sleeve, I peered through the large gaps in the wrought iron fence. Her hair, which was normally twisted neatly on top of her head, hung long and straight down her back, glowing in the moonlight. A dressing gown fluttered around her in the breeze, the silk flowing like she'd summoned the wind herself.

"Sorry, Mrs. Freeman. I didn't mean you. I was just talking to…"

"A ghost. I know," she replied too cheerily.

I gave a weak chuckle, as though I might still avoid a padded cell. However, I couldn't force my face to fake a smile. She tilted her head and waited. It was the same look she'd given students when she was waiting for a confession.

Weariness settled over me. I was tired of pretending, of running, so I dropped the act. "You can see him too?"

She shook her head. "That's your magic, dear. Not mine. I'm a garden witch."

I waited for her to laugh. She didn't.

Images of cauldrons, brooms, and wart-covered crones luring children into candy cottages flashed through my mind.

My body tensed, ready to dash into the house where she wouldn't be able to follow. Wait, that was vampires. Oh, no. Were those real too?

Mrs. Freeman held up a warning finger. "Don't look at me like I'll turn you into a frog. You're the one talking to the dead. Now, come with me. It's time we talked." She turned and gestured for me to follow.

My legs refused to move. "Where are we going?

"Inside. I've already boiled water for tea." She winked. "Don't worry. I used a kettle and not my cauldron."

Had she read my mind? I couldn't tell if she was serious or if she was teasing me. "Wait. Why can't we talk out here?"

"Because the trees have ears." She must have seen the mounting fear in my expression, because she added, "Not literally, but we don't want anyone knowing all our secrets. Come now. We have to hurry."

Swallowing, I surveyed the trees to check if they leaned inward to hear us. "Why? Are we in danger?"

"No. Because I don't want to drink cold tea."

I took in the woman I'd known practically my whole life. She appeared the same as she always had: a short woman whose presence made her seem much taller, wearing a stony expression paired with kind eyes that implied, *It's for your own good*. Yup, exactly the same. And yet she was a witch.

I belatedly recalled what she'd said. *That's your magic*. Was I a witch too?

Since there was only one way to find out, I popped over to Mrs. Freeman's for tea.

CHAPTER SIXTEEN

Seated at my neighbor's round dining table, I pretended to admire the variety of plant life that consumed the shelves, window ledges, and every other available flat surface. Secretly, though, I was searching for… I wasn't sure, exactly. Shrunken heads? Crystal balls? I didn't know the first thing about real witches. However, I was certain that if I were one, I would know. Probably.

Mrs. Freeman poured the teapot's steaming yellow contents into a floral cup. When she set it in front of me, I inspected the contents.

She must have read me like a spell book, because she said, "It's not a magic potion. It's chamomile. Good for calming the nerves." She raised her glass in a "cheers" and took a sip.

As I brought the cup to my lips, it smelled okay. Maybe I was overthinking it.

Nolan, who sat in one of the other chairs, looked unconcerned. "If Mrs. Freeman wanted to poison you, she's had twenty-seven years to do it."

Out of the corner of my eye, I noticed something black snaking across the floral rug before it leaped onto the last seat at the table.

I sloshed some tea onto the lace tablecloth as I got ready to bolt. But it was only Zelda. She laid her front paws on the table, waiting to be served. Did I smell like catnip? Why was she always following me?

Mrs. Freeman tipped some cream into a spare teacup she'd put out, as though she'd been expecting another guest, and set it in front of the cat. "We're just letting ourselves in now, are we, Zelda?"

I tilted my head. "How did you know I named her—"

But I was interrupted. By Zelda. *I would have knocked but, you know, the lack of knuckles and all.* She splayed the dark pads of her paws.

While her mouth hadn't moved to say more than "meow," I'd *heard* her as clearly as if she'd spoken the words.

Gripping my seat, I slid it back. "Did that cat talk?"

Zelda leveled me with a flat look. *I've always been able to speak, but I can control who hears me. And since, apparently, my vote doesn't count, I guess you're in the club now.* She held up her dewclaw in a thumbs-up gesture. *Congrats.*

"And she's not just a cat," Mrs. Freeman added. "She's a familiar."

The word rang a bell. "Like a witch's animal sidekick." I eyed the cat lapping up her cream. "Is that why you've been following me? Are you my familiar?"

Definitely not, thank the goddess. I'm too old for another newbie. I'm Nolan's familiar.

She was the original Zelda? I was curious how old she was, but I didn't think I really wanted to know. Besides, her age might have been the least remarkable thing about her, considering she could see ghosts—or at least Nolan.

I grabbed my teacup in both trembling hands and took a large gulp, hoping Mrs. Freeman had brewed a pot of chamomile strong enough to knock out a blue whale.

"So," I began conversationally, as though my mind wasn't spinning out of control. "I'm a witch?"

"You see ghosts, don't you?" the older woman asked. "What did you think was happening? Hallucinations?"

I shifted, uncomfortable talking about something I'd protected like a national secret for five years, pretending magic and ghosts weren't real. Meanwhile, she spoke as calmly as if she were tutoring me in geometry.

"I-I figured I'd been cursed or was sensitive to it or something. Like the way people claim they read auras or palms."

She added a dollop of honey to her tea. "Some of those people might be witches too. Most are scam artists, though."

"But I only started seeing ghosts after the accident."

Her expression softened. "That's not uncommon. Emotional events can bring out one's special abilities. I'm surprised they didn't emerge after your mom left. However, you were a bit young yet." She drifted off for a moment, like she was remembering that time. "So, you never suspected?"

"I never even knew witches existed."

"That figures," she muttered, more to herself. "Perhaps that's why your powers took so long to show themselves. Can't find what you're not looking for."

Zelda raised her head from her teacup, a cream goatee dripping from her chin. *Either that or you're a dreadful witch.*

Nolan shot her a scowl. "Zelda, be nice."

What? I'm not wrong.

"She's new to her powers. I was a novice once, too, but I remember having help." He gave her a pointed look.

The cat twitched an ear. *I decided to help you because you saved my life. I owe this witch nothing.*

"Then do it as a favor to me," he said. "Besides, you've practically moved into her house already. The way you eat, you'll owe her soon enough."

She gave an unhappy growl. *Fine. I'll do what I can. Though it's probably a waste of time.* Her yellow eyes took me in from head to toe.

An argument formed on my tongue, but I decided to keep

my mouth shut. After all, everyone in that room had far more magical knowledge than I did. Perhaps she wasn't insulting me but offering an experienced appraisal, and for all I knew, she was right.

Mrs. Freeman didn't seem fazed by Zelda's one-sided conversation, waiting until the cat's grumbling finally died down before she continued. "Anyway, I've been keeping an eye on you over the years," she told me. "That's why I moved next door after your mom left. No young witch should have to manage new powers alone. I was starting to think the magic had skipped you."

I blinked. "You mean my mom was one too?"

"Of course. It's passed down through bloodlines. I'm just sorry it took such a tragic event to bring it out."

Speechless, I stared at her. The day she'd moved in had been a devastating blow to my seven-year-old self. Living next door to the principal was like being stuck at school for eternity, but she'd only been protecting me. She knew my darkest secret and hadn't run away screaming like I had with Nolan. Instead, she understood me in a way I'd never understood myself.

I spun the wedding ring on my finger. "Nolan was my first ghost. When I woke in the hospital after the accident, he was there. I thought it had all been a nightmare and, in a few hours, I was going to walk down the aisle."

Her mouth formed an "o" as she inhaled sharply. "Oh, my dear."

"Over the following days, everywhere I turned, there he was." I held Nolan's gaze as I continued because he deserved an explanation. "When most people lose a loved one, over time, they somehow inch their way to acceptance, but I couldn't grieve and mourn and move on if you were always there. I wondered if it was the same for you. What if you couldn't move on because I was around? It felt like everyone was better off without me. So I left."

He stared at his hands. "I'm sorry you felt that way. I don't remember much from those early days. It was a bit overwhelming, and I wasn't myself. All I remember is panic, confusion, anger, and my desire to be close to you. I can see how I might have seemed a bit terrifying."

Terrifying was an understatement. It was like I'd been stuck in a horror movie, but I didn't need to rub it in. He already looked sheepish enough.

Mrs. Freeman observed the empty chair. "I take it he's here with us now?"

"Yes. He's here."

Angling her body toward the space, she gave him a sad smile. "I'm sorry for your loss, Nolan. And yours, Violet. Being back must be like reliving it all over again."

"When you found me in the garden earlier, it was the first time I've ever heard him speak. After I put on the wedding ring he bought me."

She reached across the table. "May I see the ring?"

I held out my hand, displaying it for her. It reminded me of something a gushing newlywed would do, so when she was done, I clenched my fist and pressed it into my lap.

Her mouth pursed thoughtfully. "I don't sense any magic. My guess is, because the ring held such importance to him, it acts as a conduit. It amplifies your powers to better connect with him."

"That's how my magic works?" The woman haunting the store in Paris came to mind, how I'd heard her speak once I'd touched her jewelry.

Mrs. Freeman tilted her head noncommittally. "I doubt it's the only way, but because you don't have any practice controlling your powers, it gives you the boost you need. Like training wheels. While it gets the job done, you'll eventually need to learn to ride on your own."

A humorless laugh escaped me. "I don't exactly want to become better at speaking with ghosts. I don't want to speak to them at all."

Zelda waved a paw in Nolan's direction. *Nice. Way to kick a man while he's down. Or, in his case, dead.*

Missing the days I believed ghosts were oblivious, I rubbed my forehead, where an ache was forming.

Mrs. Freeman considered me for a long moment before sighing. "I could probably help you with a spell to banish Nolan, but I don't think that's what he needs."

"What does he need?" I leaned in closer, eager to end this curse.

"The same as you, dear. Answers. Closure."

She laid a comforting hand over mine, not like a neighbor or my old principal would but like an equal. Maybe a mentor. I wasn't alone in this anymore.

"Thank you, Mrs. Freeman."

"I think it's time you called me Helen, don't you?"

"All right, Helen."

Bang. Bang. Bang.

A pounding on the door made us all jump. Helen set down her cup and sidled across the room, surprisingly swift and calculating. When she parted the curtains, she groaned before throwing open the door.

My dad stood on the other side, a fist on his hip. He looked angrier than I'd ever seen him in my life, and I suspected this wasn't about her vervain again.

"You've got some nerve, witch," he practically growled at her. "Violet, it's time to leave."

Zelda held a paw to her mouth. *Ooh, someone's in trouble.*

CHAPTER SEVENTEEN

Helen straightened her dressing gown and gestured for my dad to enter as though it wasn't the middle of the night. "Lovely to see you, Stanley. Would you care for a cup of tea?"

He didn't budge from the threshold. "No. And I'd appreciate it if you minded your own business."

Appalled, I shot to my feet. "Dad, Helen's looked out for you the last few days. Why are you being so rude?"

He barked a laugh. "Oh. It's Helen now, is it?"

The older woman huffed and returned to her tea. "Your father's never liked me. In fact, he doesn't like any of us very much after what happened with your mother."

He shook a finger at her. "Don't lump my daughter in with your kind. I told you to stay away from her. I won't have you polluting her mind."

"You can deny it all you want, Stan. It changes nothing. Keeping her from the truth all these years has only hurt her. I could have prepared her for what she is."

Dad stared at me like I was suddenly a stranger to him. "You're… You're…"

"A witch," Helen provided.

Something flared inside me, and I rounded on him. "You

knew about me, about Mom, all this time? Why would you keep it from me?"

He winced at my tone but then straightened, puffing up his chest. "I was protecting you."

"From the truth? All it did was make me feel alone and confused."

His chin lowered, and his posture sagged. "You're certain that you're…" He couldn't even say the word.

"A witch?" I asked. "Well, I see ghosts, and the last time I checked, that isn't a common skill."

Nolan stepped between my father and me, hands raised. "Violet, go easy on him. He was acting out of fear. If I remember correctly, so did you when I told you the truth."

The reminder was a slap in the face, mostly because there was some truth to it. If I were being honest, this did remind me of when Nolan had revealed his magic to me. I felt lied to, betrayed by a man I trusted inherently. This time, by my father. Why was everyone keeping things from me?

"It's completely different," I told Nolan. "I had one night to accept all of this. He's known for years."

My father took a wary step back onto the porch. "Who are you talking to?"

"Nolan," I said. "He's still here. It's one of the reasons I left. I wasn't prepared for any of this, no thanks to you."

His features warred between shock and sadness until he finally slumped against the doorframe. "I'm so sorry. We can get you help. A counselor, an… exorcist."

"What? No!" I recoiled at the suggestion. A few moments before, I'd nearly jumped at the chance to be rid of ghosts forever. Now, it felt like an inseparable part of me. It was as though my dad was asking to chop off my arm. "This is who I am—apparently. You'll have to accept that."

"I just want what's best for you," he said. "I've only ever wanted to protect you."

"I'm not a little girl who needs protecting anymore, Dad. In fact, our roles have reversed."

His head whipped back and forth almost violently. "Absolutely not. I won't let you get involved in the case any further. Let them arrest me. I'm not exactly innocent."

"But you did nothing wrong, and you most definitely didn't kill anyone. I will uncover the real murderer." I stepped closer and locked gazes with him. "And once I do, you're going to tell me about my mom and everything else you've been keeping from me."

His jaw clenched. "Violet—"

With an exasperated groan, Helen threw her hands up. "Know when to shut up and accept help, Stanley. She's more capable than you give her credit for."

At least my father didn't argue with that. "How are you going to find out who killed Wyatt Thorn if the sheriff can't?"

Okay. He had me there. "I'm not sure yet. It could be several people at this point. A whole poker table full of them, in fact."

Nolan snapped his fingers, which was disconcerting since he technically had none to snap. "What if you ask the victim himself?"

I wrinkled my nose. "Wyatt? But I wouldn't know how. You're kind of my first."

Cocking his head, he raised his eyebrows suggestively. "Ah, yes. I remember the night fondly."

"Stop." I cringed. "My dad's in the room. Don't make it weird."

Zelda howled. *I wish I had fingers to stick in my ears.* Settling for paws, she tried anyway.

Dad watched the cat's strange behavior. Since he hadn't run away yet, I assumed he wasn't in "the club," and she wasn't allowing him to hear her.

As I considered Nolan's suggestion, I absently played with my wedding band. Then it hit me. "Helen, if this ring helped me connect with Nolan, then would something of Wyatt's help me speak with his ghost?"

She gave me an almost smug look, implying, *Well done, my young apprentice.* The schoolgirl inside me practically burst with pride at the approval.

While the idea should have occurred to me earlier, I'd been a little distracted by my initiation into the magic club. There was probably a lot more to unpack, but I couldn't wallow in my mixed feelings just yet. Not when I had a murder to solve.

I wasn't certain how long someone had to touch a piece of jewelry for their spirit to leave an impact, but hopefully, something in Charming Treasures would work as a conduit. Maybe an item left behind during Wyatt's scuffle with Dad. If that failed, I didn't want to think what I'd have to resort to. Breaking into Wyatt's home? No. I couldn't do that. Right?

The uncertainty must have been clear on my face, because Nolan said, "Don't worry. You've got this."

"Thank you. And I know I do." I gave him a grateful smile then dug into the pocket of my borrowed sweatshirt. I pulled out the ring box, along with the timepiece Max had returned, and set them on the table. "While I understand you want to help, between learning about the witch stuff and talking to you after all these years, well… it's a lot to process. If I'm going to solve this thing, I need to keep a level head. I can't let myself get distracted by my own problems or my past." I cringed. "I'm really sorry for this."

Before Nolan could protest, I slipped off his ring and returned it to the slot in its velvet home. He threw back his head and released a frustrated but silent yell like I'd just hung up on him during a fight. Gritting his teeth, he stormed out through the open front door. My heart twisted painfully, but I'd have to deal with all that later.

I closed the ring box and shoved it back into my pocket. Then I swiped the watch off the table. The hunter case had popped open. An engraving on the inside grabbed my attention, and I held it beneath the chandelier to read.

It was a date. July twentieth, only four years ago.

Since my dad refused to step inside, I brought it to him. "Was this the pocket watch that was stolen from the store?"

He reached up to adjust his glasses then discovered he wasn't wearing them and squinted. "I've never laid eyes on it. If I was going to sell something pre-owned, I'd usually buff out any engravings first, depending upon its heritage, of course."

"Interesting," I said, more to myself. If it wasn't from the store, then why had it turned up in the same poker game as Roxy's necklace?

The date didn't stand out to me, especially since I'd been halfway across the world at the time. However, nothing much happened on Charm Island, so if it was at all gossip-worthy, it would have made the local paper. I'd have to check the archives.

In the quiet that had fallen over our group, I heard bushes rustle outside. We all froze, heads turning to the sound.

Peering past my dad, I scanned the front yard, but it was too dark. A steady *swish-swish* filled the tense silence, a rhythmic whisper of grass: footsteps. Someone was out there.

I dashed outside to chase after them, but my eyes were used to the bright interior. I tripped over a flagstone and nearly trampled a garden gnome. After groping my way through the front arbor, I ran into the street and searched for the peeping Tom.

Farther down the road, gravel crunched beneath shoes. Metal squeaked as a vehicle door opened and slammed shut. The motor turned over, and red taillights glowed like a pair of watchful eyes.

I raced toward it, but before I could get close, rubber chirped against pavement. The vehicle sped down the hill too quickly for me to get a good look at it. Reluctantly, I slowed to a stop in the middle of the road.

Dad caught up to me, bracing his casted arm. "Did you see who it was?"

"No. I was too late."

Flashlight in hand, Helen joined us at a composed pace, but a deep line had formed between her eyebrows. "How much do you think they heard?"

I didn't need her to tell me this wasn't a piece of gossip we wanted making the rounds. "I don't know. Where's Zelda? Can't she run after it or something?"

What do I look like, a dog? the cat griped from next to my boot. *Why don't you go fetch it yourself?*

Helen laid a hand on my back and guided me toward the house. "We can't worry about it now. All you can do is get a good night's sleep. You'll need it for tomorrow."

She was right. First things first: solve the murder and absolve Dad. Then worry about being burned at the stake.

CHAPTER EIGHTEEN

The local newspaper operated out of its original brick building at the end of Dolphin Drive. The sign above the door announced the business name in a modest Times New Roman font: *The Siren.* Judging by the peeling paint, that looked original too. Unfortunately, the sign wasn't the only outdated thing about the place. Since the paper didn't keep a website—much less post its articles on the internet—I'd had no choice but to come in person.

Once inside, I approached an antique desk that looked younger than the woman behind it. The name plate said Deloris. A variety of pencils and pens stuck out from the silver bun on top of her head. However, she didn't seem to need any of them, since she wasn't working but knitting.

She dragged her focus away from her project while continuing on with the row. "Hello. May I help you?"

I kept my voice hushed. "I would like to check the archives."

"What are you looking for?" She paused her knitting and leaned forward eagerly.

Since I didn't want anyone knowing what I was up to, I

kept it vague. "I want to research a specific date to see if any local events happened around that time."

"Oh." As though she'd hoped for something juicier, she resumed her knitting. "I can't be expected to look up every request that comes through here. You'll have to search for it yourself."

Then why bother asking? But I kept that thought to myself. "No problem. I've used the archives for a school project before."

Deloris sighed. "Things might be different than you remember. We've relabeled everything with one of those fancy label makers."

"How modern."

"Wasn't my idea. What's wrong with leaving things well enough alone? If it ain't broke, don't fix it." She grabbed a pen from the World's Okayest Employee mug on her desk and set it on an open notebook. "Sign in, and remember to sign out when you leave. I can't be expected to keep track of everyone around here."

Wondering if she was expected to do much at all, I jotted the date and time. I signed my name so even I couldn't read it. While it wasn't Fort Knox, I didn't blame the newspaper for keeping visitor records. It dealt in the most valued currency in town: local buzz.

Deloris took the pen and stuck it into her bun as though she'd forgotten she had ten others in there. What did she do with scissors?

I thanked her and walked across the large reception area, softening my footfalls as I passed by an office with a name plate for Lucy Litton. The reporter had a nose for secrets, and since my new ones had kept me up half the night, I was too exhausted for a battle of wits with her.

Thankfully, Zelda had stayed home that morning. When I'd left, she was sleeping on the window seat in the sunlight. She might not have been my familiar, but she was happy to enjoy the food and home I came with. Nolan, on the other hand, was avoiding me. While I still felt bad for shutting him out, it had freed up some head space for solving Wyatt's murder.

I released the breath I'd been holding when I slipped into the back, with no one the wiser except for Deloris. And even then, it wouldn't have surprised me if she'd already forgotten about me.

With no windows, the musty room was dark. I groped the wall next to the door and found the switch, which turned on a single flickering light bulb. It revealed rows of open shelves filled with storage boxes in various stages of decay, worsening the farther I walked into the room. I ignored them all and approached a wooden storage unit.

Each drawer was no bigger than a shoebox. Thanks to the ultramodern labels, I found the date etched into the pocket watch and pulled out an even more modern invention called the microfilm.

After I'd powered on the machine, I popped in the film roll and sat before the glowing screen. I scrolled until I was looking at the front page of the July 20 edition. The headline that day was about the deer decimating city hall's flower bed again. It called for "All Gloves on Deck" to help replant. Nothing to engrave a pocket watch over.

The next pages were dedicated to local events, geared toward the tourists that flooded the town at that time of year. Finally, I found the "Community Announcements," and a familiar face grinned back at me. It was Wyatt Thorn.

He was dressed in a three-piece suit, his face clean-shaven, hair combed neatly. Who knew the man cleaned up so nicely? Then again, I'd never seen him in anything but his dingy work jacket and, well, dead, so that wasn't hard to top.

There was no hint of a roguish smile that day. He seemed genuinely overjoyed. And for good reason—the blushing bride standing next to him looked gorgeous. The mystery date was Wyatt Thorn's wedding day.

I studied the grainy picture, zeroing in on his waistcoat. A light chain dangled from one of the buttons before disappearing into his pocket. It had to be a pocket watch. But was it the same one I had? The wedding party gift for the groomsmen might have been matching timepieces, in which case it could be any of theirs.

My focus shifted to the bride, and I realized I knew her. Tara Townsend. Or perhaps it was Thorn now.

She'd been a fairly quiet girl in school, a real dreamer, and we'd been on friendly enough terms that she invited me to the wedding. However, I'd been in Europe at the time, and only a year had passed since Nolan's death, so I'd clicked "regretfully declines" in the RSVP email.

After the big day, I checked out her photos on social media, but it was only out of curiosity, so nothing stuck out to me. Now, they were more important than ever. I automatically reached into my pocket for my phone, only to hang my head when I remembered its fatal plunge into the marina with me the night before.

On my way to *The Siren*, I'd ordered a new phone from the electronics store-slash-fried chicken drive-through, Electri-fried Wings. While it was a strange combo, in a small town, businesses had to do double duty to stay afloat. Unfortunately, it would be a week before my new cell came in. I considered running to Charming Treasures to use the internet, but our computer was ancient and barely worked at the best of times.

Once I'd shut down the machine, I put away the microfilm and returned to Deloris's desk. She'd made good headway since I'd been gone. I could see the bottom of a baby sock taking form.

When I asked if there were public computers, she pointed to the line of prehistoric monitors along the wall behind her. I hopped onto the farthest one and wasted no time signing into my various social media accounts to scroll through Tara's photos.

Consumed by my task, I didn't hear anyone approach until I heard a nasally voice in my ear.

"What are you up to, Woods?" Lucy asked.

I bashed on the mouse, minimizing the windows before she took a closer peek. Spinning in my chair, I faced the reporter, who wore a silky peacock-print blazer. The color was a shock against the somber surroundings. At least the woman was interesting, if annoying.

"My phone is out of commission," I said. "So I thought I'd come here to check emails."

Her lip twitched. "What a coincidence. I was just completing my latest article about Wyatt Thorn's murder." She hit an icon on her phone to start recording and held it up between us. "But I have a few gaps to fill first. Any last-minute comments to add?"

I recoiled. "Yes. You should probably get that phone out of my face before I tell you what gap to fill it with."

She clicked her tongue. "My, my. Such hostility. A little on edge, are we? Any particular reason?"

"Don't start with me, Lucy. Not today." I turned the chair around, hoping she'd take the hint.

Undeterred, she gripped the backrest and spun it so I faced her again. "Care to comment about your father's involvement in Wyatt Thorn's death? If not, we can always do an in-depth exposé surrounding your tragic car accident. I have to admit, I still have a few questions about that one too."

I ignored the repulsive suggestion. "You know as well as anyone else in Hope that my dad isn't a murderer."

She waved a manicured hand. "Anything's possible. Besides, murders aren't usually random, especially in a small town like this. Often, the murderer has a connection to the victim, whether it's through love, money, or revenge. And Daddy fits those last two perfectly."

I scowled. "Wyatt Thorn wasn't exactly an upstanding citizen. There might have been a lot of people who wanted him out of the way."

"That's true. Take your rugged friend, Max, for example."

I cocked my head as though I hadn't heard right. "What about him?"

"He ran in the same circles as Wyatt, and he's butted heads with the sheriff a few times. Curiously, one incident was over a break-and-enter. Sound familiar?"

The news took me by surprise. It was another reminder of how little I knew about Max these days. But his rocky history with local law enforcement also explained why he'd vanished after Wyatt's body had been found—to avoid any more scrutiny.

"Plus," Lucy continued, "I saw him fighting with Christian on the ferry minutes before you spotted Wyatt's body. He seemed unusually uptight that morning. Not unlike you right now." She raised an accusatory eyebrow at me.

Paying it no mind, I considered her theory. "But if Max was on the ferry, then he wouldn't have been on the island to kill Wyatt."

Bored with my pedestrian detective skills, she checked her nails. "I looked into it. It was just an overnight trip, so he might have been around at the time of the murder. Don't believe me? You two were once thick as thieves. Ask him yourself."

Wouldn't that be fun? My barely concealed accusations hadn't gone down so well the first time. I'd have to take Lucy's word for it, even if I was annoyed she'd gotten her hands on details I hadn't.

Swallowing my pride, I attempted to get more info out of her. "Who else do you suspect?"

She snorted. "As if I'd tell you. You'll have to read about it on my website tomorrow. Or the paper, if you're like every other dinosaur in this town. I swear, one day, I'll bring this place into the twenty-first century."

Deloris's knitting needles stopped their *click-clack*ing. "Over my dead body."

"I'm counting the days, Deloris." Lucy snatched a pen from the woman's bun and wrote a number on a sticky note before handing it to me. "Call if you change your mind about the exposé. The people deserve to know the truth." She raised her pert nose and twirled away, disappearing into her office.

The truth? The truth was Lucy Litton had never been a likable person. In elementary school, she'd been a vicious tattle-tale—in playground terms: a big meanie. High school brought her more "friends," but in a transactional sense, as though she was a wheeler and dealer of information and favors. She'd liked me as much as I'd liked her, and I'd never cared enough to try to change her mind. Then, in junior year, something shifted, and I went to the top of her hit list. She started shoehorning my name into every ugly article she wrote in the school paper, which was more like a tabloid under her reign.

While she'd never been my favorite person, it comforted me to know I wasn't the only one hunting for Wyatt's murderer. And Lucy Litton was a good reporter—not that I'd ever admit that to her. When it came to finding the truth, I trusted her more than the sheriff.

Once the door to Lucy's office shut, I turned back to the computer and resumed my search for Tara and Wyatt's wedding photos. I scrolled through all three social media platforms she was on, but there was not one picture of Wyatt to be found. That was when I noticed her relationship status: "Single."

When I brought up Wyatt's profile, his said "Married." The truth was obviously something closer to "It's complicated."

Either way, my next step was simple if not totally pleasant. While I was doing my best to avoid ghosts at the moment, now that I knew the pocket watch possibly belonged to Wyatt, it could work as a conduit to talk to him. Maybe he could shed some light on his own death.

CHAPTER NINETEEN

Since it was a cloudy day, perfect for ghost spotting, it wasn't difficult to track down Wyatt. I found him standing on the pier next to the empty ferry slip, contemplating the dark waters where I'd found his body. He was so still, he might have been a statue, except for the seagull that flew right through his head. He didn't even flinch.

At the sound of my footfalls on the wooden planks, Wyatt's head tilted in my direction, but he otherwise ignored me. At least we were alone, so I could speak freely to him. After spending so long avoiding ghosts, I wasn't in love with this plan. In fact, I secretly hoped it would fail, but I had to give it a shot.

I reached into my pocket and clutched the watch. "Wyatt?"

"What do you want?" he muttered, not registering I'd spoken to him.

I could hear him. My legs buckled with relief, and I leaned against the rail next to him.

The ferry was on a run to the mainland, so the waters below were calm except for the gentle waves carrying debris to shore. For a moment, it took me back, like the image of his floating corpse was branded onto my brain.

Rubbing my eyes, I turned to him. "Wyatt, we need to talk."

He whirled to face me, his features blurring with the sudden movement. "Wait. Y-You can hear me?"

"Thanks to this." I held up the pocket watch. "I'm here to help you." While that wasn't entirely true, I needed to play nice if I was going to get him to cooperate.

"My watch. Where did you find it?" He tried to snatch it away, but his fingers passed right through it.

"I'm more interested in how you lost it."

His eyebrows knitted together. "I don't know. I always have it on me wherever I go."

He patted his pockets as though he might find a phantom version of it on him. I assumed it was possible, since the old ferry captain stuck on the mainland still had a hole punch. But Wyatt came up empty.

Did that mean whoever killed him took it? It had turned up too quickly to have washed ashore, and there were no signs of water damage to the piece.

"Who gave the watch to you?" I asked.

"It was a gift from my wife on our wedding day."

"You mean your ex-wife?" I corrected without thinking.

"We're still married," he snarled, ghostly spittle flying from his mouth. Then his face fell, and his eyes drifted like he was trying to remember where he'd put his keys. "Or, at least, we were until I died."

Okay. I'd circle back to the wife. "Do you remember what happened the night you died?"

He shoved his gloved hands into his pockets. "Not a lot. I remember I fell a long way before hitting the water. Then weightlessness… and fear. Fear I'd be lost if I let go. I held on for as long as I could."

I struggled to follow his halting recollections, wondering if he meant a physical fall, like off the tall pier we stood on. Or was it a reference to falling off this mortal coil? I doubted he'd be able to tell the difference, so I asked, "What didn't you want to let go of?"

"My body. I held on until I washed up here."

So the ghost had used it as some sort of morbid raft? The mental image sent ice coursing through my veins. "Then what happened?"

"Once I was back on land, I felt safe. Safe but trapped."

"You mean trapped on the island?"

"No. Here." Wyatt swept an arm in a wide arc, at the world in general, as though there was another place to go.

"Have you discovered anything since then? Did you maybe overhear a conversation about your death or find any of the stolen jewelry?

"Yes." He sneered. "In your shop. Your dad had some. He tried to hide it."

"Not that jewelry," I shot back. "You left those behind when you beat him up."

I clenched the watch until the case bit into my palm. Why did I have to defend my father to this criminal of all people?

The breeze picked up, whipping my long curls around. His hair and coat remained in place like he was a hologram, unaffected by this world. I reminded myself he'd received punishment enough for his actions. Besides, it wasn't like he could hurt my dad anymore.

I took a calming breath. "I mean, have you found any jewelry you had with you right before you died? Maybe whoever killed you took it."

He pointed a shaking finger at me. "You tell me. You're the one with my watch. Did you kill me?"

"Nice try. Don't forget I'm the only one who can help you," I said, unfazed. "Someone won your pocket watch in a poker game. Ring any bells?"

His forehead wrinkled as he concentrated. "I don't play poker."

I sighed. This was getting me nowhere. But at least he'd

confirmed one thing. He would have had the pocket watch on him at the time of his death, so whoever gambled with it in that game of poker must have been involved in the murder.

Luckily, it was Friday, a popular night for poker, I'd bet. Maybe I'd start at Killer Ale. At least until Max made good on his promise to kick me out.

Wyatt had become mesmerized by the water again. I'd hoped he'd be more help. The man was able to walk through walls, so why hadn't he been gathering intel around town, tracking his murderer? Didn't he want to move on?

I poked the bear one more time. "Tell me. Were you and Tara happy?"

He wheeled on me, eyes wide, nostrils flaring. "We were soulmates. From the moment we met, Tara and I were meant to be together, and nothing was going to tear us apart. We just needed time to work things out."

Despite the fact he couldn't hurt me, I backed away. "Of course. Who'd be able to resist you? You're a real catch."

Maybe the lovebirds had been trying to reconcile before he'd died. However, if they'd been soulmates, they wouldn't have broken up at all, and he wouldn't have been stringing along another woman. Had Tara been jealous of his relationship with Roxy? Jealous enough to kill? I wanted to ask him, but something told me Wyatt wasn't the most reliable source on their marriage.

As he returned his attention to the water below, a desperate look remained etched on his face. As much as I tried to hold on to my loathing for the man, his expression tugged at something inside me.

"I'm sure your wife misses you very much."

And I was about to find out exactly how true that was.

CHAPTER TWENTY

When I arrived at Tara Thorn's shack of a home that afternoon, with its peeling paint and curling shingles, I crossed a lawn that looked like it hadn't seen a mower in years. Then again, it was mostly weeds, anyway. For a moment, I wondered if I had the wrong place; it didn't suit the girl I remembered. When the door opened, though, the woman on the other side wasn't exactly the girl I remembered but a shadow of herself.

Tara pushed the strands of overprocessed hair away from her too-thin face. "Violet Woods? What are you doing here?"

It wasn't the worst greeting, especially since I'd been the one to find her husband's body two days before.

"Hi, Tara. Do you have time for a visit?" I held out a box of fresh cupcakes from Spread the Word.

At the sight of the bakery's logo, the unease in her expression released like an elastic band. "Who doesn't have time for Alice's baking? Come on in."

I noted how she'd said "Alice's" and not "the bakery's." My bestie was practically her own brand and didn't even realize it. She really needed to open her own shop.

Tara led me through a tunnel of stacked boxes, around a mountain of stuffed garbage bags, and over a river of scattered papers to a wobbly dining table. She dug through a box on the floor and produced two plates and two forks.

"Sorry about the mess. I'm in the middle of a move."

I popped open the box of cupcakes and set one on each plate. "Oh? Where are you moving to?"

She didn't bother with the fork. Instead, she took a huge bite and answered with her mouth full. "I'm not sure yet. Far away from here. I'm finally getting out of this dump, putting it all behind me. I can't believe you came back."

Following her lead, I unwrapped my treat and dug in. "I probably wouldn't have if not for my dad."

The cupcake froze halfway to her mouth. "Right. I'm sorry about what happened to him. Wyatt was a real piece of work."

"He's actually why I'm here. I wanted to see how you're doing."

She pushed her plate away like she'd lost her appetite. "The guy had it coming to him. Everything he touched turned to garbage. If you stood too close, you'd reek too. Just look at what happened to your dad. As for me? I couldn't be happier he's gone." If that were true, her expression had missed the memo.

I set down my cupcake. "Was he always that way?"

She grabbed a box of cigarettes lying on the windowsill and slipped one out. "Mind if I smoke?"

"Go ahead." While I didn't love secondhand smoke, it was her home, and she seemed like she needed one.

She lit up. "Everything was roses at first. He had big dreams, just didn't want to work for them, and he owed everyone in town money. The man was a real fast-talker." She took a drag on her cigarette, lost in thought. "He was never a thief, though. And to attack your dad? He must have been desperate."

The photo of Tara on her wedding day came to mind. She'd been the very picture of a blushing bride with no idea of what was in store for her. "I'm sorry you had such a rough marriage."

She huffed. "Me too. But that's life, isn't it? If you don't have your guard up, it'll slap you in the face. You and I both learned that lesson." She stared at the weeds growing in the window box outside.

The Tara I remembered had been bright and bubbly. Her marriage to Wyatt had popped that bubble, chewed her up, and spit her out like old gum.

"The move might be exactly what you need. A fresh start." If anyone got that, it was me.

"Yes. We're finally free."

I blinked. "We?"

She sat straighter and leaned forward. "I have a new man. One that actually works, a real practical sort of guy. Nothing at all like Wyatt. And now that he's gone, we can finally get married and move on."

"That's fantastic." But for more reasons than one. The love triangle provided me with a new lead. "What's the lucky man's name? Do I know him?"

She pulled away. "Sorry, but we're keeping it quiet. With everything going on, the gossipmongers are already on my case. I don't want to give them any more reason to speculate."

"I understand." Not that I was happy about it. "Did Wyatt know about your new relationship?"

She snorted. "No way. He was the jealous sort, even more so after we'd broken up. He was always getting drunk and coming here at all hours of the night to beg me to take him back. Things got heated a couple of times, and I had to call the sheriff. Wyatt still had it in his delusional mind that we'd get back together, and he refused to sign the divorce papers, kept giving me the runaround."

So Wyatt's death was the only reason she could get engaged. If that didn't scream motive, I didn't know what did. But surely, with a lawyer and a bit of extra paperwork, she would have had a divorce eventually. Then I recalled Wyatt's hostility when he'd talked about his marriage. Just how determined had he been to reconcile? And how fed up had Tara been with him?

It seemed too easy, though. If my old schoolmate had been involved in his death, it was unlikely she'd be so honest about her hatred of him. Either she didn't expect to be caught or her fiancé was the real culprit.

While it was tempting to turn the visit into an interrogation, the subject already weighed so heavily on Tara that she slouched like a deflated balloon. So I asked what any woman or jeweler would in this situation. "Do you have a ring yet?"

She inflated and laid her left hand on the table. A braided three-stone ring glittered on her finger.

I inhaled sharply. It was my dad's handiwork.

"It's beautiful," I said to cover my surprise.

Instinctively, I ran a fingertip over the diamonds and the twisted platinum braid. It felt empty, too new to give me any insights into Tara's soul like, for example, if she might be a killer. If Dad had made the ring, though, he'd know who commissioned it. Then I'd have her fiancé's identity and possibly even the murderer's.

Wiggling her fingers, she watched it sparkle. "We got my man an engagement ring too."

"A lot of couples do that nowadays. Why should the woman have all the fun, right?"

She admired her ring a moment longer before stubbing out her smoke. "Look, I'm sorry to cut the visit short, but I've got a ton of packing to do."

"Of course." I tried to hide my disappointment. I'd hoped to glean more.

As we maneuvered our way back to her door, I tripped on a stuffed trash bag. It toppled over, spilling old high-school yearbooks and photo albums across the carpet.

"Sorry." I bent to tidy them.

She kicked the bag aside. "Don't worry about those. They're all headed for the dumpster."

I frowned at the pile of memories. Tara hadn't been kidding when she'd said she wanted to put it all behind her. I was about to leave when I spotted white lace and satin among the mess. Her wedding album.

Not wanting to leave empty-handed, I picked it up. "You know, despite how things ended with Wyatt, I wish I'd been at your wedding. I remember seeing some of the photos online, but they're not there anymore."

Tara hugged herself. "I deleted those a long time ago. I didn't want the reminder."

"That's too bad. I would have liked to see your wedding dress. Do you mind if I have a peek now?" I raised the album cover.

She slapped it shut again. "Take it. And when you're done, dump it in the trash. I never want to see those again."

I tried to suppress my excitement. "Will do. It was nice to see you, and good luck with your fresh start."

"I hope you get yours soon."

That made two of us.

Once outside, I walked back through the weeds to the sidewalk, fingers twitching to open the album. Unable to wait until home, I crossed the street and wandered into a green space. A bench bathed in a ray of sunlight called my name, and I sat. Checking that Tara couldn't see me from her window, I opened the album.

The first few photos were the pre-wedding frenzy: hair, makeup, dress. The youthful bride radiated hope and love. I skipped to the middle and found a group shot of the wedding party. I recognized a couple of the bridesmaids from school, but I found the groomsmen more interesting. The best man had been Christian, the deckhand. The other groomsmen included Captain Elijah—no wonder he'd seemed so broken up at Killer Ale—our new deputy, and… Max.

I quickly flipped through the rest of the pages. Nothing else screamed "clue."

A cool breeze blew over me, and I shivered. My bright spot had given way to a shadow as the sun tucked behind Sleeping Beauty. It was getting late, and I knew I should go home and have dinner with Dad, since he'd probably rather eat toast than accept something from Helen's kitchen—not that she'd offer.

After we'd had our fallout at Helen's, we didn't say much to each other. Things were still strained between us, but that was all stuff to work out once he wasn't going to prison. Besides, I needed to ask him about Tara's ring.

Snapping the album shut, I stood to leave the park but froze as gravel scuffed nearby. I searched for the source and saw a man approach Tara's house. Tall and broad, he had his jacket hood pulled up, concealing his face. Could it be her new fiancé?

I ducked behind a bush and peered between the branches just sprouting new leaves. Not the perfect camouflage, but nothing about my investigation had been perfect so far. I watched as the man knocked on Tara's front door. A moment later, she opened it and gave him a hug before ushering him inside—a warmer welcome than I'd received.

The guy stepped inside and turned to shut the door. That was when I caught a glimpse beneath his hood. If it had been a stranger, I couldn't have picked out his features in a police lineup, but I'd have recognized that face in the dark. It was Max.

The air whooshed out of my lungs. I sank to my knees in the damp grass. Moisture seeped through, but I didn't move.

Was Max Tara's new fiancé? His presence couldn't be a coincidence. I thought back to the moment before my midnight swim off his boat and the impression my attacker's bracelet had given me. The woman had been bitter and determined. That fit Tara, all right. However, if he was engaged to her, then why gift Roxy the necklace, even if it was only a friendly gesture?

Max kept popping up everywhere I turned. As much as I wanted to deny it, he had to be involved in this mess. Was that why he'd been so insistent I stop investigating? Rather than looking out for me, he might have been trying to keep me from learning the truth.

I massaged my temples. The answer felt so close and yet so jumbled, like a puzzle I'd dumped on the table. Most of the pieces were there, but I hadn't put it all together yet. Though my dad could fill in the one piece that might make the picture clearer: the identity of Tara's fiancé. I just hoped it wasn't Max Nicolas.

CHAPTER TWENTY-ONE

On returning home for dinner, I quizzed Dad about Tara's ring. Unfortunately, he couldn't recall who'd ordered it. That left the store records as my only shot at finding the answer. The name would be on file, giving me my next and most likely suspect. As I headed back downtown, Zelda tagged along, insisting it was out of boredom and definitely not because Nolan had asked her to look out for me. Despite her surly attitude, I didn't mind the company, though I was still getting used to chatting with a cat—especially one that talked back.

By the time we arrived, the sun hid below the horizon. Only a blush of pink clung to the sky, making it hard to see if I was about to trip on the uneven boards. Of course, Zelda had no problem seeing where she was going, but she didn't bother to warn me before I snagged the toe of my shoe and stumbled. As though reading my mind, the lampposts flickered on.

All the stores had long since closed, their interiors dark, windows shuttered. During the off-season, the place felt like a ghost town at the end of the day. At the thought of an entire town inhabited by ghosts, I shuddered.

As I approached the promenade, there was one store with its lights still on and the door wide open. When I got closer and saw which one, the grilled cheese in my stomach turned sour—hey, at least I hadn't ordered in. It was Charming Treasures. Was it another break-in?

Wishing I had a phone to call 911, I picked up my pace. When I got closer, something shifted in front of the store. Nolan. Well, half of him. The shaft of light spilling from the open door erased his bottom half.

"What on earth is going on?" I whispered.

He shot me a withering look.

"Right." I winced. "No ring. Sorry."

I raced up the steps and stormed into the store, only to be blocked by a man. I jumped and staggered back onto the little porch. My fists clenched at my sides as I prepared for a fight.

Jason stepped into the doorframe, blocking my view. "Sorry, Vi. I can't let you in."

My mouth popped open. "Excuse me? This is my family's shop. What are you even doing here? Who let you in?"

He held out a paper between us. "The sheriff has a warrant. We spoke with your dad ten minutes ago. I'm surprised he didn't let you know."

"I don't have my phone right now."

Tinkling and banging drifted from the rear of the shop. My chest tightened at the sounds. I imagined Sheriff Reed tossing around jewelry and scuffing polished finishes, his dirty fingers leaving smudges on the diamonds and other gems.

Zelda slithered between Jason's legs. *Well, I don't need a warrant.*

"Hey, furball!" Jason made a *psst* sound. "Get out of here."

I crossed my arms. "Don't yell at my cat."

Zelda flashed her teeth at me. *I am not your cat.* Then she disappeared into the back.

While Jason was distracted, I tried to peer around him. He adjusted his stance again, easily filling the gap with his broad frame.

I stamped my foot like a tantruming two-year-old. "Jason, please."

His "I'm on duty" mask fell away, face creasing with pity. "You know I can't. This is my job. But don't worry. When the sheriff finds nothing, he'll be forced to give up on your dad, and everything will return to normal."

My stomach turned. That was the problem. What if he did find something? The sheriff was a bloodhound on the scent. He would keep searching until he found that secret floorboard.

I tugged on a lock of my hair until it hurt. "There are some really expensive, irreplaceable things in that store. They need to be handled delicately, with gloves and velvet cloths. You can't just toss them all together."

A crash from the back made me wince. I felt like a bottle of soda shaken to the limit, and I was ready to pop.

Jason laid a gentle hand on my shoulder. "The sheriff won't damage anything on purpose, but I'll remind him to be careful. I promise. In the meantime, you should go. This is only going to upset you."

Annoyed at being treated like a porcelain doll, I shook him off. "Oh, please. As if you really care."

He flinched. "How can you say that? Of course I care. It's still me. I'm your friend."

"Then, please, help me." I hugged myself tight. "Tell me anything you can about Wyatt Thorn, about who might have wanted to kill him. A partner in crime? His wife? Her new fiancé?"

He squinted at me, running a thumb along his lower lip. "New fiancé?"

This was clearly news to him. Good thing I'd started investigating on my own. The sheriff hadn't even uncovered that much.

Jason held up his hands. "Look, even if I could give you information, there's nothing to tell. I haven't run with those guys for a few years. I left that shady lifestyle, and all who went with it, behind me. I'm a man of the law now."

I sighed, knowing he was telling the truth. He had turned into Mr. Upstanding Citizen, as annoying as that was at the moment.

Once again, I tried to peek around him and failed, so I stomped back down the steps. Instead of going home like he'd told me to, I paced outside the shop, glaring through the open door as though my real witch power was shooting laser beams from my eyes. Maybe I had the ability to turn the sheriff into a frog. Was that a thing?

Nolan watched me with an expression I knew too well. It said, "You won't do any good here. Stop being so stubborn."

Yeah, yeah, yeah. I knew he was right. Now that they had the warrant, if they found those jewels, it would only be a matter of time before the sheriff inspected them and put the pieces together—incorrectly, of course. My dad would look guilty, and so would I. I'd tampered with evidence, lied to an officer of the law, and aided a "criminal."

If only I could check our records for the name of Tara's fiancé, I'd be able to crack this thing, but it didn't look like that would happen now. There was a lot less time to solve the murder than I'd hoped, and I should have been using it wisely, talking to more people.

The antique post clock on the promenade said it was nine o'clock. Was it too early to visit Killer Ale?

Ignoring the *I told you so* look on Nolan's face, I spun on my heel to head that way, nearly running into somebody.

"Sorry, I—" The words died on my tongue as I saw who it was.

Mayor Abernathy's lips curled into a sneer, their fullness highlighting his distaste for me. "Violet. Beautiful evening, isn't it?"

I bet it was beautiful for him. He was getting exactly what

he wanted. I leveled him with a cool stare. "I'd answer if I believed you actually cared."

"Come on. After everything that's happened, I thought we'd be good friends."

I wanted to laugh. Friends? We'd almost been family, and now, he was showing up to celebrate my father's downfall. "All right, Quinton. I can call you Quinton, can't I? We are friends, after all. And as my friend, you can put a stop to this." I thrust my arm at the shop.

He stroked his tie, smoothing out invisible wrinkles. "I'm afraid I can't do that. In fact, I'm here to lend a hand."

"Of course you are. You've been eyeing Charming Treasures for a while. But I'm curious how badly you want it. Enough to sic the sheriff on my dad? Enough to cause the trouble in the first place?"

Nolan raised his arms like, *What are you doing?*

Typical. He'd always sided with his father.

The mayor chuckled. "That's quite an imagination you've got there. I'm just here doing my civic duty. Since this is my town and my ancestors essentially built it, I've taken an interest in the architecture of the original buildings. Did you know many of these shops have hidden doors and secret hiding places that even the owners aren't aware of?"

My insides turned icy. I wrangled my expression into an unreadable mask like I had during so many Abernathy dinner parties. "So you've come to aid in my father's destruction. How… friendly of you."

"If your father's innocent, he has nothing to worry about, does he? And the sooner we find the answers, the sooner we can all move on with our lives. If anything, you should want me to help."

I shook my head. "Why are you doing this? Do you hate me so much that you're willing to take my father down to get back at me?"

"Hate you?" He tilted his head, eyebrows raised innocently.

"After what happened to my son? After you argued with him, made him chase you all over town, and then he lost control and drove off a cliff? How could I hate you for that?" His usually aloof expression suddenly twisted. "I despise you."

The fury rolling off him had me backing up a step, but I straightened and stood my ground. "We never would have been in that car, having that fight, if it hadn't been for you. So make sure you save some of that blame for yourself. Just leave my dad out of this."

He took a step toward me, forcing me to crane my neck to continue our heated staring contest.

Jason popped out of the shop then. "Everything okay out here?"

For a moment, I thought he'd intervene, but Abernathy shooed him away. Jason ducked his head and slunk back inside like an obedient dog.

As the mayor held my gaze, his eyes narrowed and… changed color? No. It was like a light glowed behind them, electricity building during a power surge. In the near-dark around us, it was mesmerizing.

A crash from within the store pulled my attention away, and I scowled. Jason stepped out again, cringing with his palms turned up. When I spun back to Abernathy, his cool mask had fallen into place again.

What on earth was that?

Was the mayor magical after all? While I'd hoped it wasn't the case, Helen had said it passed through bloodlines, and since Nolan had been a warlock, it only made sense his father was one too.

I glanced at my fiancé, who shrank away from his father almost fearfully. And he was a ghost, impervious to harm. That wasn't a good sign.

"Now, if you'll excuse me, I have to go." The mayor straightened his already pristine tie. "I only want what everyone else wants in this town. Justice."

Did he mean for Wyatt or Nolan? I lost my chance to ask as he entered Charming Treasures and confidently strode into the back room. A moment later, Zelda shot out the door, streaking toward me.

He found your stash, she said. *What are you standing around for?*

When I didn't move, she hissed, startling me out of my frozen state. I began to leave, but Nolan didn't follow. He shifted from foot to foot, torn between coming with me and staying with his father. Wasn't that the story of our relationship?

Shaking my head, I left him behind, practically sprinting toward Killer Ale, now desperate for the truth. There was no time left for finesse, for sneaking around and teasing out clues. It was time I went all in to weed out the real killer or hope he'd reveal himself.

Miss Levelheaded who?

CHAPTER TWENTY-TWO

Ollie the Orca regarded me as I paused beneath him to catch my breath. His toothy grin flashed with warning. I might have been about to make a huge mistake, but I was out of time and options. Thrusting back my shoulders, I marched inside.

The moment the door swung open, the bouncer jumped off his stool. "I'm not supposed to let you in here."

I didn't bother pretending he had the wrong woman. It was tough to be inconspicuous when you had blazing-red hair. "And why not? I'm just here for a game of poker."

He stiffened. "We don't play poker here. We're not licensed for gambling," he said like he was reciting lines. "You must be confused."

"Right." I winked.

When a dark shadow darted between our legs, he leaped back. "And there are no cats allowed in here."

"Not my cat," I said at the same time as Zelda expressed a similar sentiment only I could hear.

With a growl of annoyance, the bouncer bent to snatch her up. She snickered as she jumped from floor to table to bar, teasing him with her twitching tail.

At least she was on my side, even if Nolan wasn't. Then

again, she might have been doing it simply because she enjoyed being annoying.

Not wasting the diversion tactic, I strolled confidently past the bar. I was afraid the bouncer would tackle me at any second, so I didn't look back as I pushed open the double doors to the rear of the building.

Old stained-glass lights dangled over multiple pool tables, and music thumped from a jukebox. A woman chalking the tip of her cue eyed me before she sent the balls flying with a loud *clack*. I ignored her and scanned the room. An arcade game belted out tinny music in the corner, and two men played foosball. No poker tables. However, if they weren't licensed for it, they wouldn't be playing out in the open, would they?

A door with a red Private sign caught my attention. It might as well have said, "Nothing interesting going on in here, especially if you're the sheriff." I marched straight for it and burst into a tiny, dimly lit room.

At my sudden entrance, a half dozen pairs of eyes glanced up from their cards to fix on me—five men, one woman. At least one pair was familiar: Max's. The way they burned with outrage didn't fill me with the warm fuzzies, though, especially since he was one of my lead murder suspects.

Seeing him there, hanging out and playing cards as though my entire world wasn't falling apart, was a slap in the face. Maybe we hadn't been friends for a while now, but didn't he care? Didn't our history mean anything to him? Anger reared inside me like a wild animal.

Christian was there, too, just as I'd hoped. Perfect. Two birds with one gemstone.

I slammed the door shut and locked it. While it would give me only a few extra seconds, I needed all the help I could get.

Max tossed his cards onto the table. "What are you doing here?"

"I'm here to do some betting." Which wasn't a lie. Everything was riding on this play, and it was going to take a lot of bluffing.

He crossed his muscular arms. "It's a private game."

I grabbed an empty seat, plopping into it before I fainted from anxiety. Everyone stared at me, their expressions incredulous. I plowed on, not giving them the chance to recover from their shock.

"I'd like to bet that Christian was in on the jewelry store robbery with Wyatt Thorn. Then he killed him so he wouldn't have to share."

Christian jerked back. "What? Who are you? The neighborhood watch?" He said it with a sneer, but there was an undercurrent of fear to the reaction. "Wyatt was my friend."

I planted my elbow on the table, accidentally knocking over a few colorful chips before resting my chin on my fist. "Tell me, how did everything go south? Did you fight about the jewelry?"

He shoved away from the table and got to his feet. "I don't have to listen to this."

Ignoring the fact my heart was doing a tap dance, I pressed on. "Did he double-cross you or plan to throw you under the bus, so you killed him and took all the stolen goods for yourself? Maybe that's why you're planning to skip town."

Next to me, a man with a beard so long it was braided threw his cards down on the table. "You're leaving? You owe me money, you snake."

Max hauled me out of the chair. "Come on. Let's go, before you join Wyatt."

I wrenched out of his grip and wheeled on him, my fury jerking free of its leash. "Why? Are you going to kill me, Max? Maybe you were the one who murdered Wyatt." I tilted my head in Christian's direction. "Is that what you two were fighting about on the ferry? The money he owed you from the robbery?"

Christian yanked his yellow rain slicker off the back of his chair. "I'm outta here. I've got a boat to catch."

The woman who'd been watching in silence finally spoke, her half-lidded gaze fixed on me. "I suggest you find somewhere else to be, too, sweetheart."

Max's hold on my arm tightened. Not painfully, just firm, maybe even protective. "Don't worry," he told the group. "I'll take care of this."

Again, I tore away. "You'll do no such—"

Max bent in front of me. Before I could back away, he threw me over his shoulder and hauled me out of the room.

I tried to kick my legs, but he locked them beneath his arm. So I banged on his back, screaming bloody murder as he carried me through the bar. I might as well have been hitting a brick wall. All it did was hurt my fists.

Once outside, he set me down beneath Ollie. "Have you lost your mind? I told you not to come back here."

I flicked my hair away from my face. "Why? What are you trying to hide? Did you really kill Wyatt? How else would you get a necklace he stole from our jewelry store? Not to mention, you had his pocket watch."

"That was his?" His features slackened with surprise before he brushed it off. "I told you I won them playing poker."

"So you say. Or did you take it off his cold, dead body?"

Max lowered his chin to his chest, and when he looked back up, the same hurt I'd seen on his boat was back. "You really believe I had something to do with any of this? With your father's injury or letting him take the fall for murder? Do you think so little of me?"

A surge of guilt choked me, but I swallowed hard and forged on anyway. I'd come to get answers, not to make friends. "What were you doing at Tara's house today?"

"You followed me?" Then he raised a hand. "You know what? I don't care. And I don't need to answer your questions. I told you to let me handle this." He turned to leave.

Grabbing his arm, I tried to stop him, but it would have

been easier to stop a bull. I circled him to block his path. "Why? Because you're hiding something?"

He suddenly gripped me by the shoulders. "Because I'm trying to protect you!"

I balled my hands into fists and groaned. "I am sick and tired of people protecting me from the truth. One way or another, I am going to get my answers."

"Well, you won't find them here."

As he glowered at me, I didn't so much as blink. The bar door opened as someone left, letting a slice of light out. The reflection caught Max's eyes. For a second, they almost glowed, not like the mayor's had but the way an animal's would in headlights. Fear tickled my spine, something instinctual.

What? Was the whole town magical?

It had to be the stress of everything, a trick of the light, but I recoiled anyway. Seeming satisfied, Max stalked off into the night, toward the marina.

Desperation welled inside me, and I called out after him. "And here I thought we were friends."

He turned to look over his shoulder. "Friends don't turn their backs on friends. Not the way you did. You say I've changed, but you're the one who's not acting like yourself. This isn't you. At least, not the Violet I remember." Then he disappeared into the night.

Rage roiled through me, at him, at myself, until it felt like my skin was on fire. I tugged my zipper so my jacket hung open, and I stumbled around the corner. Gripping the deck rail, I leaned over it in case I lost my dinner. The cool ocean air washed over me, along with the last few minutes.

Max had been right. This wasn't me. At least not who I wanted to be. I'd acted like a complete fool, yelled at him, made a few enemies in that poker room, and may have put a target on my back. And where did it get me? I was no closer to finding Wyatt's real murderer.

This whole time, I'd been keeping my distance to avoid

getting caught up in my past and the heavy emotions that came with it. But that meant alienating the very people who might have helped me if I'd only asked. Now, it was too late. I'd let my emotions get the best of me again. The last time I'd done that, Nolan died. And this time, because of me, my dad was going to jail.

"That went well," a smooth voice said.

Startled, I wheeled around. Leaning against the bar's clapboard siding, partially hidden in shadow, was Roxy. Maybe it wasn't too late after all.

CHAPTER TWENTY-THREE

On edge, I eyed Roxy, who stood next to the building, wrapped in shadows. Was she spying on me? How much of my argument with Max had she heard?

I hugged myself. "What are you doing out here?"

"Taking a break. Back when I smoked, this was my hiding spot, but I quit a while ago. I still find the sound of the waves peaceful, though." She shoved away from the wall and stepped into the light. "Looks like you've been back in town for all of five minutes, and you're already making friends."

Sighing, I slumped against the railing. "That's me. A real people person."

I was tired of seeing enemies everywhere I turned, tired of keeping my distance with everyone, acting sneaky and clever—not that I ever managed the last one. I'd been trying to solve the murder with one toe in the water. It was time I dove in headfirst and got real with someone.

"I'm trying to uncover Wyatt's murderer."

Roxy pursed her lips. "So that's why you came in here the other night. To quiz me."

"I was here to get answers, but I didn't know who you were until we started talking. I'm trying to prevent my dad from being arrested for a murder he didn't commit. And you did say you taught Wyatt a lesson. What did you mean by that?"

"Whoa." Hands raised, she took a step back. "I meant that I poured beer into the gas tank of the stupid classic car he loved so much. I certainly didn't kill him."

"Because you were out of town?" I asked, not convinced. "That's what you told Elijah. Where was it you said you went?"

"I didn't." Her narrowed eyes roamed over me until her posture relaxed. "All right. I'll tell you, if only so you lay off me. My boss can't find out, though."

I showed her my right palm like I was taking an oath. "My lips are sealed."

"You know that new resort on the west side of the island?" She waited for my nod before continuing. "I was out there because they offered me the position of bar manager. They wanted to get my input and give me an orientation to the place. It's a bit out of the way, so I stayed in one of the finished rooms for a couple nights."

"Congratulations on the new job."

"Thanks." Roxy joined me at the railing. "Their grand opening isn't for a while. They keep having setbacks, so I need this Killer Ale gig until they open. If my boss found out I was going to quit on him, he'd fire me on the spot." She pulled out her phone and tapped the screen a few times before turning it to face me. "Here. Have a look."

It was an email with the resort logo at the top. It did read like an offer of employment.

She took the phone back. "Still don't believe me? I have all the text messages about the meeting with date stamps."

"I believe you. Your secret's safe with me. So if you didn't kill Wyatt, I don't suppose you have any idea who did."

Staring at her fingers as though she wished there were a cigarette in them, she picked at her cuticles. "I don't. But he was getting off the island that night. He texted me, begging me to come with him. Imagine, after everything, he thought we'd actually run away together."

She gave a hollow laugh, but I wondered if part of her regretted not going, like if she'd been there, maybe he'd still be alive. It was more likely that she would have shared his fate. However, I found his sudden about-face strange. Wyatt had been obsessed with his ex-wife, but when he was skipping town, he'd called Roxy. Was that because Tara had already shot him down? Or perhaps he found out she'd moved on with someone else and Roxy was a backup.

"What time did you get those texts?"

She opened something on her phone and held it out again. "Read them for yourself."

I didn't move to take it. "Why are you showing me all this?"

"Because I don't like games," she said pointedly. "And I don't like being accused of killing my ex, so let's get it all out in the open so you won't be back to harass me at work."

"Fair enough."

As much as I didn't want to invade her privacy—any more than I already had—the truth was more important. I took the phone and scrolled through the texts. There were no responses from her, just a series of messages from Wyatt that worsened as they went on.

WYATT

Baby, I made a mistake. I want to be with you.

Don't let what we had go to waste. Come with me.

We can be together.

Blah, blah, blah.

I didn't read them all. It felt like an intimate peek into her life I didn't deserve. Plus, his attempts to manipulate her sickened me, so I skipped to the last one.

My mind returned to my conversation with his ghost. While I hadn't understood the recounting of his death at the time, now, it made more sense. *I fell a long way before hitting the water.* Like from the deck of a ferry.

Whoever murdered him had been on the ship. Since Max went to the mainland for the night, he could have been on that last run. Or perhaps Christian had been working and was there for Wyatt's final voyage.

I gave Roxy her phone back. "Is the sheriff aware of this?"

"No. My dumpster fire of a love life didn't seem like key evidence." She gnawed on her lip as she read the texts again. "But I guess this might be important."

"It might make all the difference in the world." As in, it would prove my dad didn't kill Wyatt because he hadn't been on that ferry. And it was all because I'd simply asked Roxy. If I'd stopped being so distant with people sooner, I might have uncovered the killer already. Maybe it wasn't too late, though.

"Thank you for showing all of this to me. And for what it's worth, I'm sorry."

She nodded, and I headed for the promenade. I still wondered if she'd shoved me off Max's boat, but I'd gotten my answers, and I was afraid to push for more. Besides, the sheriff needed to know this new information ASAP. Too bad I didn't have my phone, and something told me the bouncer wouldn't let me back inside to use the bar's.

Behind me, the music drifting from Killer Ale grew louder as the front door opened and a shout floated out. "And stay out!"

A moment later, Zelda was muttering next to me. *You eat one person's battered fish, and it's the end of the world. Humans.*

I shook my head but didn't chastise her. She'd earned herself the treat. "Thanks for the help."

You're in a better mood, she said. *Though, I didn't mind all the kicking and screaming you did on your way out. I hadn't expected dinner and a show tonight.*

"That's because while I don't know who the killer is, I think I can prove my dad is innocent."

As we neared the promenade, I spotted Nolan standing next to the jewelry store. He must have been waiting for me because the shop was dark. Clearly, Reed and Abernathy had found what they'd been hunting for.

Armed with my new theory, I started for the sheriff's office, but movement along the cliff-edge boardwalk caught my eye. I squinted, trying to make out the retreating figure in the dark, but they were too far away. Then they passed beneath a light post, and a bright color flashed. A yellow rain slicker. Christian.

Now that I wasn't surrounded by a table of intimidating poker players, I registered what he'd said. *I have a boat to catch.* The ferry.

Did my questions hit too close to the truth? Was he making a quick exit now that I was onto him?

I checked the time on the post clock. It was ten p.m. Across the harbor, the ferry was just pulling into the terminal, lit up like a Christmas tree in the darkness.

Before I'd consciously made the decision, my legs steered me in that direction. I'd make sure that ferry didn't set sail with Christian on it, even if I had to beg the captain or rally the passengers like a neighborhood watch gang. He wasn't getting away.

CHAPTER TWENTY-FOUR

As I snuck along the boardwalk that hugged the uneven harbor cliffs, whitecaps crashed against the rocks below, shushing me like I was being too loud. *Shhh. Shhh.* Or maybe that was just my fear talking. I didn't want Christian to notice me tailing him before we were surrounded by other people. While I was determined to make him answer for his crimes, I didn't have a death wish.

Nolan followed soundlessly behind me. Well, soundless to my ears. I knew him well enough to assume he was telling me off for doing something so dangerous. Still, I was glad for the company.

Zelda kept pace with me, padding softly along the weathered boards. *I don't like this.*

"It will be fine," I told her. "People on the ferry will help me, and I can use someone's phone to call the sheriff."

I mean, because I hate water.

I shot her a look as we passed beneath a flickering lamp-post. "You live on an island."

Because I choose to stay on land and avoid the water. The eye roll was audible in her voice.

It was such an inane conversation, but it eased some of the tension building behind my ribcage. "So don't go for a swim."

She hissed irritably. *The ferry is on the water.*

"So is the island, but we're not wet now."

I don't know, she grumbled. *You look awfully damp to me. You're not the one wearing a fur coat, and yet you're sweating from every pore.*

Snorting, I didn't bother with a comeback. I was short of breath, and the thick fog rolling in wasn't helping. It felt like inhaling soup. But worse, it made keeping Christian in sight even harder. By the time I rounded another bend in the path, he'd vanished. Either the mist had swallowed him or he was a faster walker than I was. Some spy I made.

Keeping my ears strained for someone lurking in the shadows, waiting to jump me, I pressed on. When we finally reached the terminal, and I stood safe and sound in front of the ship, I breathed a sigh of relief. That is, until it dawned on me that I was alone. The ferry had shut down for the night.

Cautiously, I made my way along the passenger walkway and approached the gate. It was still open. Surely, the staff wouldn't leave it like that for the night. Maybe someone was still around to talk to. Boarding, I eyed the dimly lit decks, wondering whether to check out the vessel or run in the opposite direction.

Silence settled around me, thick and choking as the fog. Was I wrong and Christian hadn't been heading that way after all? Maybe he'd veered off at one of the many other paths I'd crossed after I lost sight of him. He might have meant a different boat, like a friend's recreational craft. Or what if he was here, and I was alone with him?

I recalled the way I'd goaded him in the bar. If I ran into him now, there would be no help, no witnesses. What had I been thinking?

"You're right," I told Zelda. "This is a bad idea."

When she didn't respond, I searched behind me. She was back on the shore, planted firmly on solid ground. At least she'd made it closer than Nolan, who'd joined Wyatt in his favorite spot on the pier. I was the only reckless one on the boat.

It was clear I should have gone to the sheriff's office first. I'd just been so desperate to make sure Christian didn't slip away. That and maybe a tiny part of me had wanted to take him down myself to show Reed up. Turned out my pride didn't always make the best decisions.

Making my way back to the passenger gate, I moved to disembark, but before I could, a large figure blocked my path.

I backpedaled, a scream building in my throat until recognition caught up. It was Captain Elijah.

The air left my lungs in a grunt. "Oh, hi."

"Hello." He squinted at me. "What are you doing here so late?"

"I, well…" I struggled to invent a story that didn't sound as wild as "I was chasing bad guys. You know, I'm all about busting crime in my spare time."

"Earlier today, I realized I lost my favorite watch on the trip home. I was hoping it was on the ferry or in your lost and found. But I see you're shut down for the day, so I'll come back tomorrow."

He scratched his beard. "Nothing has been turned in as far as I know. It's no bother if you want to poke around. No one is here, and I was just on my way to Killer Ale. I'll wait while you have a look."

For the first time, I noticed he wasn't wearing his captain's uniform but casual jeans and a fleece jacket. The man certainly wasted no time getting to the bar.

Gnawing on my lower lip, I weighed my options. Christian obviously wasn't there, and I was anxious to alert the sheriff before he got away. But if Wyatt had been killed on the ferry, maybe there was still evidence to prove it, like the rope used to strangle him. It would clear Dad's name without a shadow of a doubt, and Elijah's offer gave me the perfect excuse to investigate before anyone had time to tamper with it.

"Actually, that would be great, thanks. I won't be long."

"Don't worry about it," Elijah said. "If you're looking for me, I'm going to hit the head." Absently playing with the ring on his finger, he slipped into the restroom by the luggage rack.

When the door closed, I climbed the stairs to the passenger deck. It was dark. A phone would have been handy, mostly so I could tell someone where I was, but it would have been nice for the flashlight function too. At least the periodic flashes from the lighthouse on the headland illuminated the surrounding fog.

As I searched the outer walkway, I found rope everywhere, coiled in lifeboats and wrapped behind ring buoys. When I came to the base of the stairs where I'd witnessed the fight between Max and Christian, I slowed. There was one more deck: the captain's helm.

Wyatt's retelling of his death came back to me. *I fell a long way.*

Pushing my shaking legs forward, I started up the stairs to where I'd first met the captain. What was it he'd said? *I run a tight ship, so nothing happens without me knowing.* If Wyatt had been on his way to the mainland the night he died, Captain Elijah would have known.

An image of him twisting his ring appeared in my mind's eye. People commonly fiddled with jewelry when not used to wearing it. Since it was on his fourth finger, maybe he'd recently gotten married or, perhaps, engaged. And while there was a whole town full of potential fiancées, my thoughts went straight to Tara. If he was her mystery man, it would explain her being so tight-lipped about the relationship.

According to Lucy, murders were often over love, money, or revenge. What if it hadn't been about the jewels at all but love? Maybe Wyatt learned Tara had moved on with his friend and groomsman, of all people, and that was why he suddenly wanted to leave the life he was trying so hard to get back. It would support my theory about why he'd asked Roxy to leave the island with him.

As I scanned the deck, I really didn't want to find anything incriminating. But, unable to help myself, I kept moving forward. I felt too close to the truth to stop now.

Hanging on the back of the door to the captain's helm was a standard orange ring buoy. The rope attached to it wasn't neatly wrapped like all the others but hung messily. The lighthouse's beam passed overhead, illuminating a red stain on the rope. It could have been rust. However, when I touched it, dark liquid smeared onto my skin.

Wet? Surely, if it was Wyatt's blood, it would have dried already.

My attention flicked to the space next to the captain's helm, where he'd invited me to stand when we'd arrived at the island. Not wanting to but needing to, I peered over the rail. There was no deck or walkway below us. It was a straight fall into the chilly waters.

Another round from the lighthouse reflected off the water. Something was down there. For a moment, I thought I was having a flashback to when I'd discovered Wyatt's body. White-knuckling the rail, I stared until the light beam came around again.

A yellow rain slicker.

Christian was floating face down in the water.

Nauseated, I staggered away. My breaths came in gulps as panic sank in. I had to get out of here. Now.

Erratic movements next to the ship drew my attention. Two figures jumped and gestured wildly from atop the pier next to the ferry. Wyatt waved his arms frantically, while Nolan thrust his arm over and over, pointing at me.

No. Not at me. Ice flooded my veins. *Behind me.*

I wheeled around in time to dodge an oar aimed at my head. It came so close that my hair shifted from the force.

Elijah stumbled as though he'd put his full weight behind

the attack and hadn't expected to miss. He meant business. With a determined expression, he raised the oar again.

Out of instinct, I grabbed the buoy and threw it at him. It glanced off his temple, and I dashed for the stairs. But he recovered quickly and blocked me. There was no way out.

As he raised his weapon high, I gripped the rail, ready to take my chances in the water with Christian's body. I was about to jump when a loud yowl pierced the fog.

Something dark leaped through the air, landing on Elijah. He howled and recoiled, but it clung to him like Velcro. Between feral spitting and snarling, I heard Zelda's voice in my head.

Take that. And that!

Her claws flashed as she swiped at his face over and over. Crying out, he dropped the oar to fight her off.

I picked it up and jabbed it into his belly, trying to push him overboard. He doubled over but barely budged. Releasing a frustrated yell, he finally got a hold of Zelda. With a fling of his arm, he threw her over the side of the ferry.

As her shadowy form sailed over the railing, she yelled, *You owe meeeee—*

Splash.

"Zelda!"

I wanted to see if she was okay, but then Elijah wheeled on me, dabbing at the bloody claw marks on his face.

Turning, I ran for my life.

CHAPTER TWENTY-FIVE

As I fled, the captain's heavy footfalls thundered on the boardwalk behind me. I swore I felt his hot breath tickle the back of my neck. Every aching muscle in my body screamed for me to stop, but I feared what would happen if I did. And while Nolan and Wyatt kept pace with me, they wouldn't be much help, so I focused on putting one foot in front of the other until, finally, the promenade lights glowed ahead.

"Help!" I yelled, hoping my voice would carry across the marina to Killer Ale.

Maybe someone was lingering outside. Roxy, perhaps, on another break. I strained to listen for a response, but my plea was met with silence. Even if someone was standing outside, the music's heavy bass would likely drown out my cries. I had to get closer.

As I veered toward the bar, I glimpsed Elijah out of the corner of my eye, closing in on me. Nolan tried to tackle him, his ghostly form tumbling right through his body. If only I had Zelda's vicious claws again, but she was still MIA. While I didn't think a little swim would hurt her, I was still worried.

Elijah slowly cut me off, herding me toward the marina. It

was the last place I wanted to be at this time of night, with so many dead ends and barely any light to see by. But then I felt his fingers brush my jacket sleeve.

Too close! No choice.

I descended the stairs two at a time. Footsteps thundered behind me. I dared a look over my shoulder to find Elijah on my heel. At the top of the stairs, Nolan and Wyatt stopped short, too afraid to go near the water. I was on my own.

The path narrowed and split off into various docks and berths. My feet found their own way as though guided by instinct, following a route to the safest place I could think of: Max's sailboat.

Less than an hour ago, I'd accused him of being a murderer. Yet I felt the same way I had five years before when I ran into his arms, scared and confused. I'd known he'd be there for me. Would he be there for me now? Or had I alienated him to the point he'd given up on me?

Friends don't turn their backs on friends.

Oh, the many layers of irony.

As I maneuvered the series of walkways to his boat, the choppy water lapped at my feet between the wooden planks. I skidded on a wet patch and nearly somersaulted into the water. A post halted my tumble. Righting myself, I kept running.

The *Crescent* emerged from the fog, bobbing at the end of the dock. I just hoped my old friend was home.

"Max!" I screamed with my last ounce of breath.

Then, I was tackled from behind.

We sailed over the end of the dock and plunged beneath the water. My muscles went rigid from the shock of it. Elijah grabbed onto me, and his heavy body weighed me down.

I kicked and flailed until my shoe connected with his soft middle. His hold slackened, and I struggled to the surface and gasped for air.

Elijah was on me in an instant. He gripped my hair and

clothes, pushing me back under. Scratching, clawing, kicking, biting, I fought for sips of air before he forced me down, over and over.

He was going to drown me. I'd be another body found in the morning, long after he'd made a break for it. The water wrapped around me like a cold, heavy blanket, the undulating waves rocking me to sleep.

Something caressed my leg. A fish? Then it bumped me harder. It was *way* too large to be a fish. I twisted to face it, but everything was dark.

My childhood fear of sharks seeped into my brain. I was about to be murdered, and yet the idea of my corpse being consumed by a shark was too much to bear.

Whatever it was brushed against me as it swept past. Elijah's warbled cry carried through the water. He jerked and let me go.

I shoved away from him and broke the surface. Between coughs and sputters, I gulped sweet air until my head cleared. I needed to get to safety.

Swim.

Blinking saltwater out of my eyes, I peered through the fog and searched for the dock. We'd floated so far away, and my limbs felt heavy. There was no way I'd make it. I was still going to drown or get eaten by a shark. Whichever came first.

The water swelled as something large cut through the waves, heading straight for me. *Eaten. Definitely eaten.*

I tensed, bracing for sharp teeth to pierce my skin, but when the creature connected with my stomach, I was nudged backward. It swam against me, picking up speed as it pushed me closer to the dock. Closer. Closer.

When I was within reach, I grabbed the edge of the wooden planks. With a flick of its tail, my rescuer swam off. I didn't understand what had happened or why it hadn't hurt me, but I wasn't about to stick around in case it changed its mind.

Arms shaking, I pulled myself along the wooden structure until I found a ladder. I hauled myself up it and collapsed onto the dock, shivering and panting.

While I gathered the energy to move, my fishy friend made life difficult for Elijah. Its fin poked out of the water, making tight circles around him as he thrashed to avoid it. Suddenly, he jerked and let out a high-pitched scream.

Still, despite the creature's efforts, Elijah worked his way to the dock. He'd reach it in moments, and I didn't have the energy to outrun him again. Somehow, I got to my feet and searched for something to fight with—anything. All I found was a pile of netting heaped at the end of the dock.

I dragged it over. As his hand slapped down next to my boot, I shoved the net so that it flopped on top of him. He disappeared beneath the water under its weight.

A second passed, then another, until I worried I'd drowned him. When he resurfaced, gasping for air, the net was still draped over him, the rope digging into his cat-scratched face. Though the net was weighted and he looked about as tired as I felt, it wouldn't keep him trapped for long.

I turned to run but skidded to a stop when I found I wasn't alone. Relieved to have help, I nearly cried until I saw who it was. Wyatt.

What was he doing so close to the water? Not even Nolan had followed. But Wyatt hardly seemed to notice his surroundings. He scowled down at his old friend and, probably, murderer.

So used to his mopey "what's the point?" expression, I saw the moment something snapped in him. His jaw clenched with determination, and he leaped over the side of the dock. Instead of passing right through Elijah as Nolan had, he wrapped his arms around his neck in a kind of ghost piggyback ride. He was actually touching him.

Elijah's grip on the dock slipped, and he dipped beneath

the water again before finding purchase on a post. He hugged it for dear life.

Was Wyatt somehow heavy? Or was his hold on Elijah a metaphorical weight upon his literal shoulders? Either way, the captain was struggling.

"P-Please," he sputtered. "Help me. I can't get out. And there's something in here with me."

Help him? He had to be kidding. But if he died, what kind of justice would that be for Wyatt or Christian? Plus, tying up loose ends would be messy for my dad. As much as Elijah deserved a taste of his own medicine, he needed to answer for what he'd done.

My teeth chattered so hard I worried they'd shatter, and my body was racked with shivers. However, I couldn't lose my advantage over Elijah or leave him to get help in case he drowned or got away.

I knelt on the dock and tried to control my trembling voice. "N-Not until you tell me everything. I'll start for you. You were in on the robbery with Wyatt, then he discovered you were with his wife. Am I right so far?"

A wave slapped him in the face, and he spat out a mouthful of water. "His ex-wife."

I hugged myself tight as my shudders intensified. There was no point in wasting time arguing with him. "So when he tried to take off with the jewelry, you killed him and took the stolen goods, including his pocket watch."

Elijah bobbed his head, partly nodding and partly shiver-ing. "The last run is always quiet. N-No one was around to see me strangle him and t-toss the body overboard."

"How could you? He was your friend."

Perhaps Wyatt sensed there was no way out for his murderer, or he wanted to hear the answers as much as I did, because he relaxed his hold. Elijah's struggling seemed to lessen, and he breathed a little easier.

"Some friend," he spat. "He mistreated his friends and family, his wife, everyone. He had it coming to him."

The words sounded familiar. "Tara told me the same thing. Did she know?"

"Sh-She's clueless, in more ways than one. Sweet girl but naive. Needed someone to take care of her, to protect her from users like Wyatt."

Did he really think a killer was better for her?

Farther down the dock, a figure materialized from the fog, approaching at a run. It was Max. When he saw me, he slowed and heaved a sigh. I couldn't help but notice he was soaking wet.

Not done with Elijah yet, I ignored him. "Was Christian involved in the robbery too?"

"Y-Yeah." Another bout of tremors gripped him. "F-Fool started gambling the jewelry away, including Wyatt's watch. Tonight, he came to me in a panic, said you were onto him. Wanted to turn himself in."

"And you couldn't let that happen." I sat back on the dock, the truth weighing on me. While I might not have killed Christian, I'd sent him running to his death.

"Now, get me out before I become shark bait!" By the way his body convulsed, hypothermia was likely to kill him first.

Max helped me to my feet. "I'll pull him out. Get on my boat and change into any clothes you want. My phone is on the table. Call the sheriff."

I jerked my head up and down, but my teeth were chattering too much to answer.

On my way to the *Crescent*, I paused to watch Max help Elijah out of the water. Fresh blood spread across the captain's jeans from large gashes in the fabric. Whatever had been in there with us clearly hadn't found him edible, but that hadn't stopped it from taking a few samples.

Wyatt, still clinging to Elijah's back, released his viselike hold, but he didn't fall into the water. Instead, he drifted back, as light as a feather, a look of glorious relief on his face. In a flash, he dissolved and floated away like bright fireflies that only I could see.

Wyatt Thorn had moved on, and now, so could my dad and I.

CHAPTER TWENTY-SIX

Stepping off Max's boat, I pulled up the hood of his jacket, snuggling deeper into its warm fleece-lined embrace. The sheriff's questioning had lasted so long I'd thawed out, and my shivers were subsiding. The three sweaters and two sweatpants I'd borrowed from Max might have helped too. I was acquiring quite the collection of his clothing.

I wanted to thank him for everything and tell him I'd be back to return his clothes, but a quick scan of the marina told me the investigation outside the boat had wrapped up. The place was deserted, so I headed for the promenade. I'd barely taken three steps before something wet and black skittered across the dock toward me.

"Zelda! There you are."

Without warning, she launched herself into my arms. Taking the jacket zipper between her teeth, she yanked it down then climbed inside for body warmth. I tensed as moisture seeped through the layers of clothes between us.

Who leaves their cat to drown? she hissed.

I braced an arm beneath her like I had a bizarre baby bump. "I thought you weren't my cat. And in case you didn't notice, there was a murderer chasing me." I rubbed the shivering lump to warm her. "But thank you for what you did. Really. I owe you my life."

No. She sneezed three times. *You owe me fish. I want salmon. And tuna. Lots of tuna. Halibut, tilapia, flounder, cod…*

As I listened to the expanding list, impressed by her knowledge of fish, I zigzagged along the docks and walkways. When my shaking legs finally climbed the last step to the promenade, the flurry of activity surprised me.

The EMTs, who'd already given me the thumbs-up, were helping Elijah onto a stretcher. At least I assumed it was the disgraced captain because the person was wrapped in so many blankets. Once the safety rail locked into place, the sheriff handcuffed him to it. Between Zelda and… whatever had been in that water, he had a few wounds that needed attention before they put him behind bars.

Nolan was waiting for me. His brow creased with something between relief and guilt, probably because he hadn't been able to follow Elijah and me down to the marina. However, I was certain the only reason Wyatt had managed it was thanks to blind rage and a desire for vengeance. I still didn't understand how a spirit was able to touch the living, much less drag them down. I had a lot to learn about ghosts because, apparently, it was kind of my thing now.

Despite the late hour, the usual busybodies had congregated, including most of Killer Ale's customers. Word got around fast. I was glad I'd called Dad after hanging up with the sheriff. The last thing he needed was to hear about the events secondhand and worry or rush down to the promenade.

When I didn't see Max anywhere in the crowd, I started for home. I didn't get far before someone thrust a phone in front of my face. It was Lucy.

She put on a professional demeanor like we'd never met before. "Care to comment about tonight's activities? The way the sheriff tells it, you're quite the hero." Her long lashes fluttered as though resisting an eye roll.

When I didn't respond, she jiggled the phone, and the bracelet around her wrist jangled. Familiarity hit me. Not by the sight of it but in a sixth-sense way.

"Actually, I have a question for you. Why were you sneaking around Max's boat?"

Instead of denying it, she raised her chin. "I might ask you the same thing. You see, I witnessed Max threaten Christian on the ferry, so when Wyatt's body washed up soon after, the timing seemed a little suspicious. I had to find out if there was a connection, so I decided to poke around Max's boat."

"And shove me into the water? That's reasonable." Then again, after my earlier outburst at the bar, who was I to judge what was reasonable?

Lucy relented with a tilt of her blond head. "I'd say it's because I didn't want to get caught, but a part of me found it satisfying."

"I hope it was worth it, because now, I won't give you the satisfaction of a story." Okay, so while an interview had never been on the table, a little torture was the least she deserved.

"Fine." She pouted. "I'll just have to weave together my own tale, whether you like it or not."

I snorted. "Let's face it, I wouldn't have liked it anyway."

Disdain crossed her face as she gave me the once-over, her eyes pausing on the cat poking its head out of my jacket. "You're so weird, Woods."

No argument here, Zelda quipped.

Jason approached with long, slow strides, thumbs tucked into his belt. He looked to be enjoying the dramatic conclusion of the case. "Call it a night, Lucy. Vi's been through enough. She doesn't need you badgering her. And this is an active crime scene."

Lucy sniffed. "I don't see any yellow tape."

Zelda's chest vibrated against mine as she purred. *I like her.*

Why didn't that surprise me?

Jason shooed the reporter away. With a throaty sound, she

spun and marched toward the Killer Ale crowd, probably to patch together a story I'd regret.

I flashed him a grateful smile. "Thanks for that."

As he spotted the furry head poking out of my jacket, he jerked back. He opened his mouth as though he wanted to ask then must have changed his mind. "I should be thanking you. What you did tonight was nothing short of amazing."

"I just wish I'd figured it all out before someone else died."

He turned to watch the EMTs load the stretcher into the back of the ambulance. "I used to run with all three of them. Wyatt robbing a store isn't so far-fetched. And Christian had a tendency to spend more than he made, so he might have been desperate. But I wouldn't have expected this from Elijah. He had a good job and was a respected member of the community."

"So why do you think he did it?"

With a shake of his head, he turned his back on the ambulance. "He said the job paid well, but the Charm ferry is privatized, so his opportunities on the island were limited. He wanted more. To get out."

I'd gotten out but for different reasons. In the end, the island wasn't the problem. A person can run from their ghosts for only so long.

Jason thrust his chin at the patrol vehicle parked nearby. "Once we get Elijah sorted out, I can come back and give you a ride home."

Exhaustion weighed heavily on me, and I didn't want to wait that long. Before I could turn the ride down, I was interrupted.

"I can walk her home," Max said, climbing the last step from the marina.

As he strolled over to me, I noticed he'd swapped his wet clothes for a thick flannel coat and jeans. His damp hair hung in long, loose tendrils around his handsome face. The sight stirred something inside me, and I forced myself to look away.

Jason wedged himself between us. "I'd like to make sure she gets home safe."

I frowned at his tone. Why wouldn't I be safe with Max? I recalled our confrontation outside the bar, the strange way his eyes glowed and my instinctive fear. But that had been the stress of the moment, my imagination on the prowl for wickedness or more magic where it didn't exist. I trusted him even if Jason didn't.

Max blinked lazily at the deputy, as though he were staring at a harmless bunny. "She'll be safe with me. Besides, I imagine you still have work to do, you know, being a hero and throwing old friends in jail." He gestured to the ambulance that was driving off. "It wasn't too long ago you were the one in handcuffs."

Jason raised his chiseled jaw. "We all have to answer for our mistakes at some point. I've atoned for mine. Yours will eventually catch up to you."

Taking a step closer, Max gave him a smile—and not the warm and inviting kind. "Is that a threat? Because if it is, you know where to find me."

As the two men closed in on either side of me, Zelda's head poked out again. *It reeks of testosterone around here. I might have to jump back into the water to wash off the stench.*

I didn't disagree with her. Feeling like the meat in a sandwich, I stepped out of the way of their staring competition. Not that they noticed, since I was a lot shorter than them.

When they didn't back down, I cleared my throat. "Maybe Max is right, Jason. You have a lot of work to do. It's only a fifteen-minute walk. I'll be fine." And the truth was, I wanted to talk to Max alone.

Jason inhaled, ready to argue, but the sheriff called out to him. "Deputy Swan, you coming?"

"Be right there," he called back and then turned to me. "I'll check on you tomorrow to see how you're doing." He narrowed his eyes at Max before he sauntered to the sheriff's SUV.

With a hand on my shoulder, Max guided me away from the promenade almost protectively. As Nolan followed, I threw him a sideways look that asked, *What was that?*

He turned his palms up. I wasn't sure if it was because he didn't know or couldn't tell me without my ring. Ghost charades weren't my strong point.

Once the sounds of the crowd and flashing lights faded behind us, I said, "So, you and Jason seem thick as thieves."

Max let his arm drop away from me. "We haven't been on the same side for a while now."

Same side? I recalled my conversation with Lucy. "A little birdie told me you've been in some trouble with the law."

We passed beneath one of the antique lampposts, and the light illuminated his expression, but it was still unreadable. "Not really. The law is just looking for trouble with me."

"Is there a difference?"

"The difference is I've done nothing wrong. Your knight in shining armor just has it in for me."

I snorted. "He's not my knight. This damsel saved herself tonight, without the help of a man, thank you very much."

Zelda's muffled meow drifted out from under my jacket. *How's that for appreciation?*

"Okay," I relented. "I had a little help from a cat and a fish."

Max eyed the round lump I patted like a pregnant belly, a genuine smile on his face. "When they call them fur babies, you know they don't mean it literally, right? And I might need you to expand on the fish thing."

"It could have been a friendly neighborhood shark." I huffed, too sore and tired to laugh. "But I'm still waiting for a few explanations from you. Like why were you so wet earlier?"

While it wasn't the most important question on my mind, I thought I'd kick things off with an easy one. However, he rubbed the back of his neck, avoiding my gaze. I hadn't expected that one to stump him.

"I, um, heard you call out in the marina. I came running but tripped and tumbled into the water."

"My hero." I laughed until I noticed his left eyebrow twitch. He was lying, but I didn't call him on it. "Well, thanks for looking out for me. You know, after everything."

He considered me for a moment as we walked in silence. Eventually, his posture relaxed. "To answer your earlier accusations—"

"Suspicions," I corrected, as though that made it any better.

"Christian and I argued on the ferry because he owed me a lot of money for carpentry work. As for my visit to Tara, I told you I'd take care of things, so I started digging on my own. That's also why I was playing poker tonight, to question the gang more subtly than you did."

My mouth fell open. Even after all these years, he hadn't turned his back on me. I didn't know what to say.

Nolan, Max, and I fell into a familiar rhythm, strolling side by side like we used to. When we entered the dark residential streets, Nolan appeared totally solid, almost human. It felt like old times.

Finally, we arrived at my house, and I paused at the gate to my yard. While my bed beckoned to me, who knew when I'd get the chance to talk with Max alone again? Well, except for Zelda and Nolan's presence.

"Max, I'm so sorry I accused you. I should have known better. You're not that kind of guy."

There was so much more I wanted to say, like I was sorry for walking away all those years ago, for not writing or calling. But that was a much bigger conversation and one we couldn't have in front of Nolan.

"That's okay," he said. "You were desperate to prove your dad's innocence. That's one quality I've always admired about you, your loyalty to the people you love. I just wonder why you stopped being loyal to me."

He looked as though he really wanted an answer. I wished I could tell him everything, about Nolan, that I was a witch, and all the reasons I'd left the island. I'd never meant to abandon Max. Guilt had prevented me from staying in touch. Not because he'd professed his love for me but because it had meant more than I'd ever be able to admit.

"I don't deserve you, Max." I knew I should have added "as a friend," but it wasn't what I meant.

"That could never be true." This time, his eyebrows remained fixed in place; he earnestly believed it.

Did that mean I hadn't permanently screwed everything up between us? A spark of hope warmed my cold insides. Was there still a chance to make things right? Maybe a chance for… us?

A smile tugged at my lips. Then I remembered Nolan standing there, and I dropped my focus to the pavement.

No. It's impossible.

I felt like a terrible person for even thinking about it. So I shoved the idea back down—deep down—where it had lived since the terrible night of the accident. When I met Max's gaze again, my expression must have been too hard, too resolved, because he nodded and backed up.

"I'm glad you're okay, Violet."

I watched him walk away until the darkness swallowed him. Keeping my face wiped clean of emotion, I turned for the house, to where my dad was probably waiting up for me. I wondered if Max and I would ever work things out, leave the past behind, and rediscover our loyalty to one another. Maybe as friends. Maybe more?

CHAPTER TWENTY-SEVEN

When I woke the next morning, my ragged backpack was staring at me from the corner of my room, where I'd been living out of it since my return. It stuck out among all my familiar things: my patchwork quilt, the antique dresser that had a collage of photos stuck into the mirror's frame, the chair I'd been rocked in as a baby. I couldn't look at it anymore. It was time to unpack.

After dragging my stiff and aching body out of bed, I shuffled around my room. As I tossed clothes into drawers and my simple travel bling into my old ballerina jewelry box, contentment warmed me. Sure, not much had changed since I'd run away from Charm Island. Nolan was still a ghost, his murderer at large, and his parents dead set on making life difficult for my dad and me. However, it wouldn't get any better if I left again.

I would fix everything, and not just Nolan's unsolved murder. I'd save my family's business, be there to help Alice achieve her dreams, and rebuild my friendship with Max. But first things first: I needed to be on time for work.

Remembering how chilly the store was, I grabbed a cardigan from my dresser. Sitting on the polished top was my wedding ring box. I only hesitated a moment before opening it.

No more running away.

I plucked the ring out of its home and slipped it on. It felt strange to wear it on my left hand, so I switched it to my right. A perfect fit.

Before I could stare at it too long, the doorbell rang. I rushed to answer it since Dad was still sleeping.

As I'd expected, he'd waited up for me to get home from my showdown at the marina—well, I found him sleeping in his recliner. I'd given him the highlights: bad guy caught, Dad a free man. I skipped some—okay—*all* the details about my involvement, rushing to the part where we both said goodnight and stumbled to bed.

When I opened the front door, Jason and an exhausted-looking sheriff were standing on the other side. The scruff on the older man's face and dark circles around his eyes told me he hadn't been home to shower or sleep. Jason wore a similar five-o'clock shadow but must have been running on adrenaline because he bounced on the balls of his feet.

I eyed Reed warily, half expecting him to arrest me for no other reason than spite. "Morning, Sheriff."

"Miss Woods. I came by to thank you for your help last night. Without your involvement, Elijah might have gotten away or killed somebody else before we caught him. You did both me and the town a big service."

I had to hand it to him. His tone was earnest, if a little too practiced. How many times had he rehearsed the speech before coming to say it to my face?

"You're welcome," I said. "But we both know I didn't do it for you. You didn't give me much choice."

"Thanks all the same." He looked past me. "Is your dad around?"

Instinctively, I blocked the doorway. "He's sleeping in."

"I'll come by again later, then. I just wanted to let you know I've put Charming Treasures back in order and returned all the evidence."

"And the stolen pieces?" I asked, worried about two in particular.

As if reading my mind, he said, "I'm afraid the art deco rings are still missing, and a few others, including a ruby necklace."

That one wasn't missing. I knew exactly where it was, but I didn't tell him that. Roxy could keep it since I wouldn't have solved the case without her. Hopefully, it would bring her luck with the next man she dated—was it unfair that I didn't want it to be Max?

"Well, Jason. Let's get out of her hair." Reed tipped his hat at me. "Thanks for your time. I apologize for any inconvenience this case has caused either of you."

"You were just doing your job," I said almost convincingly.

As I watched the sheriff and his deputy walk across our yard, something sparked a memory from the night I'd learned the truth about my heritage from Helen. Before I could think it through, I chased after them.

At the sound of my footsteps, Reed turned. "Yes, Miss Woods?"

"Now that the case is closed, do you plan to stop lurking around in the middle of the night and eavesdropping on our conversations?"

I didn't know what made me say it. It paid off, though, because shock seized his weary features before they rearranged into a mask again.

He stared me down as if considering whether to lay the truth on me. "That wasn't for this case. It was for another one."

Stunned, I waited for further explanation. Instead, he tipped his hat again and made for his patrol vehicle.

What other case? Was it to do with Nolan? Maybe he was following his suspicions about my involvement with the car accident. Or was it something far worse? If he was just trying to get in my head, mission accomplished.

I tucked the worry away for later. I'd talk to Helen about it the next time we had tea. Maybe it was more of a meeting. Were we like a coven now?

Jason lingered behind. "Don't mind him. He's just sore that you solved his case."

"Somebody had to," I muttered. "It wasn't like he was going to do it."

Squinting against the morning sun, he considered the SUV and lowered his voice. "I might be biased, but the sheriff's a good man. He's always been kind to me. Even when I didn't deserve it. If not for him, I wouldn't have turned things around and gotten this job."

His softened expression told me Reed was more than a mentor to him. After all, Jason had grown up without knowing his father, and his uncle, Alice's dad, was absent during his childhood. The sheriff was likely the closest thing he'd ever had to a father figure. However, just because he'd given Jason a break didn't mean he'd afforded me the same luxury.

"Maybe so," I said. "It still doesn't change the fact he swept Nolan's investigation under the rug. I was in that car, and it was no mechanical malfunction. Somebody must have tampered with it. Nolan was murdered. I know it."

Jason weighed his next words carefully. "There must be a reason the sheriff deemed it an accident. He wouldn't have ignored clues. People wanted answers, most of all Nolan's father, *the mayor*," he emphasized like I needed the reminder. "And the sheriff might be the law around here, but everyone knows Mayor Abernathy has the real power."

I gnawed on my lip, my focus growing distant. "You're absolutely right. That means the sheriff didn't sweep the case under the rug. The mayor did." But why would Nolan's own father do such a thing?

"Whoa." Jason raised his hands. "That wasn't my point. I'm saying that if Mayor Abernathy believed there was even a remote chance his son was murdered, the man would have pushed for the truth until every resource in town had been exhausted."

But I wasn't listening anymore, because I was onto something. They'd dropped the case too soon. As rich as Mayor Abernathy was, he hadn't even recovered the car from the bay to have it inspected. Why didn't he want answers? Or did he have them already, and calling off the case was his way of burying them?

The sheriff honked the horn and rolled down the side window. "Deputy, I can hear my bed calling."

Jason backed away. "Anyway, I'm relieved you're okay. And I'm glad you're back. This town wasn't the same without you."

"Thanks. I'm glad I'm back too." And despite everything that had happened since my return, it was the truth.

Deep in thought, I went back inside. The smell of coffee and a steady *clink-clink* of a spoon twirling inside a mug told me Dad was awake. I slipped into the kitchen to put on the kettle, but he'd already done it for me.

He took in the bruises and scratches on my face, along with a variety of other minor injuries. "I know there's a lot you're not telling me about last night." He held up a hand before I could speak. "And I'm not ready to hear it, at least until I've finished my coffee. I'm afraid to know how much I owe my freedom to you."

"Don't worry," I said. "The sheriff will probably fill you in later."

"For now, I'm just glad you're okay."

He pulled me in for a hug. I sank into it, aware of how close I'd come to having iron bars between us. However, when he drew back, tension still tugged at the wrinkles next to his eyes. We hadn't talked things out since Helen's, but the way he was looking at me said we were done ignoring the elephant— or witch—in the room.

"I know you want answers about your mom and everything else." He wiggled his fingers to encompass all the magical stuff. "And I'll tell you. I promise. I may need time, though."

Dad had been through a lot recently. After my own escapades, I needed some time too. "That sounds fair."

"I'd always planned to tell you, but I also knew it wasn't an easy life. It hadn't been for your mother. I figured that if you weren't aware, weren't expecting it…" He shrugged. "Then, the older you got, the harder it was to come clean."

"Well, the magic is here to stay, and the more I know, the easier my life will be. While I don't need answers right away, I'll need them soon."

He nodded solemnly. "I promise."

Checking the clock, I discovered time was slipping away, so I made my tea to go. I didn't want to be late opening the shop. Sure, there were bigger things going on than jewelry, but at the moment, it was all I wanted to worry about. I craved the familiarity and routine of work and the possibilities that came with creating again.

On my way out the door, I spotted Zelda dozing on Dad's recliner and called back to the kitchen. "I almost forgot. Do you mind feeding the cat? I promised her lots of fish."

Dad poked his head out into the hall. "So we have a cat now?"

"Apparently."

Zelda yawned and repositioned herself. *I'm not your cat. Think of me more as an esteemed houseguest.*

The spring weather was crisp, but the sun warmed my face as I strolled down the hill to the town center. Before long, I sensed a presence next to me. While it was too sunny to see ghosts, there was a subtle difference in the air, like I was looking through glass.

"Hello, Nolan."

"I see you're wearing the ring," he said. "Feel like talking to me now?"

Sighing, I tilted my head in his direction. "I'm sorry. About everything. I was so determined to avoid all the big emotions that came with being back, just like I have been for the last five years. I've always told myself it was best for everyone if I kept my distance, but I was lying to myself. It was only what was easiest for me."

Nolan was quiet for so long that I thought he'd left. Then, he finally spoke. "I don't blame you for staying away so long. It must have been a shock to see my ghost after the accident."

"It wasn't just seeing your ghost. It was seeing you every-where—in town, in my house, even in my room, all the while screaming at me." I shivered at the memory. "You were in so much... pain. That's the only way to explain it. I'm sorry I left you like that instead of staying and solving your murder. But no one would listen, and I was at my wits' end. I just felt so helpless."

"Well, for what it's worth, you did a great job solving Wyatt's murder, even without my indispensable help," he said humbly. "The best part was watching the sheriff admit you saved the day."

I narrowed my eyes. "Were you spying on me?"

"I wanted to make sure Reed wasn't giving you any more trouble."

"What would you do if he was? Haunt him?"

He sucked in a breath. "Ouch. That stereotype offends me as a ghost. I do more than haunt, you know. I also loiter and tarry. Sometimes, when I'm in the mood, I even dally."

I pressed a hand to my chest. "My apologies. But please don't dally with the sheriff. I can't help but think of the British meaning of the word."

We fell into a comfortable silence. When we reached a bend in the road, Hope City stretched below us, with Prosper Strait glittering like diamonds beyond that. While I'd seen a lot of amazing views during my travels, nothing was sweeter than the sight before me.

"So, how long before you leave again?" Nolan asked.

"Actually, I'm going to stick around. I'd like to dig into our accident, figure out what really happened. But if I do, you have to promise to give me some space to get used to all this magic and ghost stuff."

"Okay, okay. I guess I have been a little clingy. I promise to back off, but it'll be nice to have you around again."

While I couldn't see him, I heard the grin in his voice, and I mirrored it. It wouldn't be easy atoning for my absence or learning about my magic. But for us to move on, I had to try if we were going to stand a ghost of a chance.

THANKS FOR READING

I hope you enjoyed reading *Engrave Danger*. If you have a moment, I would be so grateful if you could leave an honest review online. Reviews are crucial for any author, and even just a sentence or two can make a huge difference. I genuinely appreciate your time and support.

Thanks!
Casey

ACKNOWLEDGMENTS

The idea for this series has been haunting me for years, ever since I was inspired by my time on Haida Gwaii and met all the folks who welcomed me to that bewitching place. I'd like to give a special shout-out to George Pattison for your kindness and all our adventures together and Ralph Nelson for the breathtaking paragliding experience. Even after all these years, those magical memories still have me under a spell.

Conjuring up ideas in a whole new genre can be rather spooky, so I'm grateful to Claire Taylor and Becca Syme for their guidance and encouragement along the way. Of course, no one would want to read this thing without my fantastic editors, Dayna M. Reidenouer, Jennifer Herrington, and Kimberly Husband who are real wizards at exorcising my errors. And I can't forget my beta team, who helped me get the earlier versions of the book into shape. Claire Merle, Diana Garcia, Sandra Anderson, Veronica McIntyre, Kathy Brenzi, and Heather Kelley, you're real gems!

Finally, to my husband, who holds down the fort while I disappear into my office and become a ghost at times, thank you from the bottom of my soul.

ABOUT THE AUTHOR

Casey Griffin spent her childhood dreaming up elaborate worlds and characters. Now, she writes those stories down. As a jack-of-all-trades, her résumé includes registered nurse, heavy equipment operator, English teacher, photographer, and pizza delivery driver. She's a world traveler and has a passion for anything geeky. With a wide variety of life experiences to draw from, she loves to write stories that transport readers and make them smile. Casey lives in Southern Alberta with her family, and when she's not traveling, attending comic conventions, or watching *Star Wars*, she's writing every moment she can.

CASEYGRIFFIN.COM